MAYA

makes a

MESS

RUTU MODAN

MAYA
makes a
MESS

A TOON BOOK BY

RUTU MODAN

TOON BOOKS IS AN IMPRINT OF CANDLEWICK PRESS

ABDO Spotlight

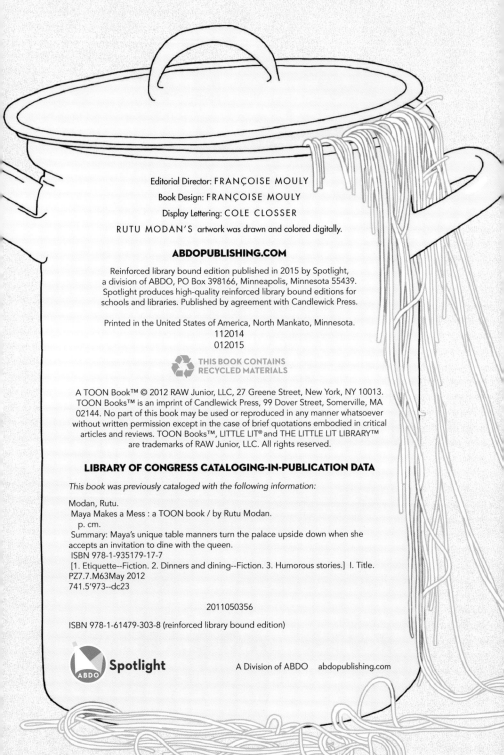

**For Hilel,
who can never have too much pasta.**

Editorial Director: FRANÇOISE MOULY

Book Design: FRANÇOISE MOULY

Display Lettering: COLE CLOSSER

RUTU MODAN'S artwork was drawn and colored digitally.

ABDOPUBLISHING.COM

Reinforced library bound edition published in 2015 by Spotlight,
a division of ABDO, PO Box 398166, Minneapolis, Minnesota 55439.
Spotlight produces high-quality reinforced library bound editions for
schools and libraries. Published by agreement with Candlewick Press.

Printed in the United States of America, North Mankato, Minnesota.
112014
012015

THIS BOOK CONTAINS
RECYCLED MATERIALS

LIBRARY OF CONGRESS CATALOGING-IN-PUBLICATION DATA

This book was previously cataloged with the following information:

Modan, Rutu.
Maya Makes a Mess : a TOON book / by Rutu Modan.
    p. cm.
Summary: Maya's unique table manners turn the palace upside down when she
accepts an invitation to dine with the queen.
ISBN 978-1-935179-17-7
[1. Etiquette--Fiction. 2. Dinners and dining--Fiction. 3. Humorous stories.] I. Title.
PZ7.7.M63May 2012
741.5'973--dc23

2011050356

ISBN 978-1-61479-303-8 (reinforced library bound edition)

Spotlight
ABDO

A Division of ABDO   abdopublishing.com

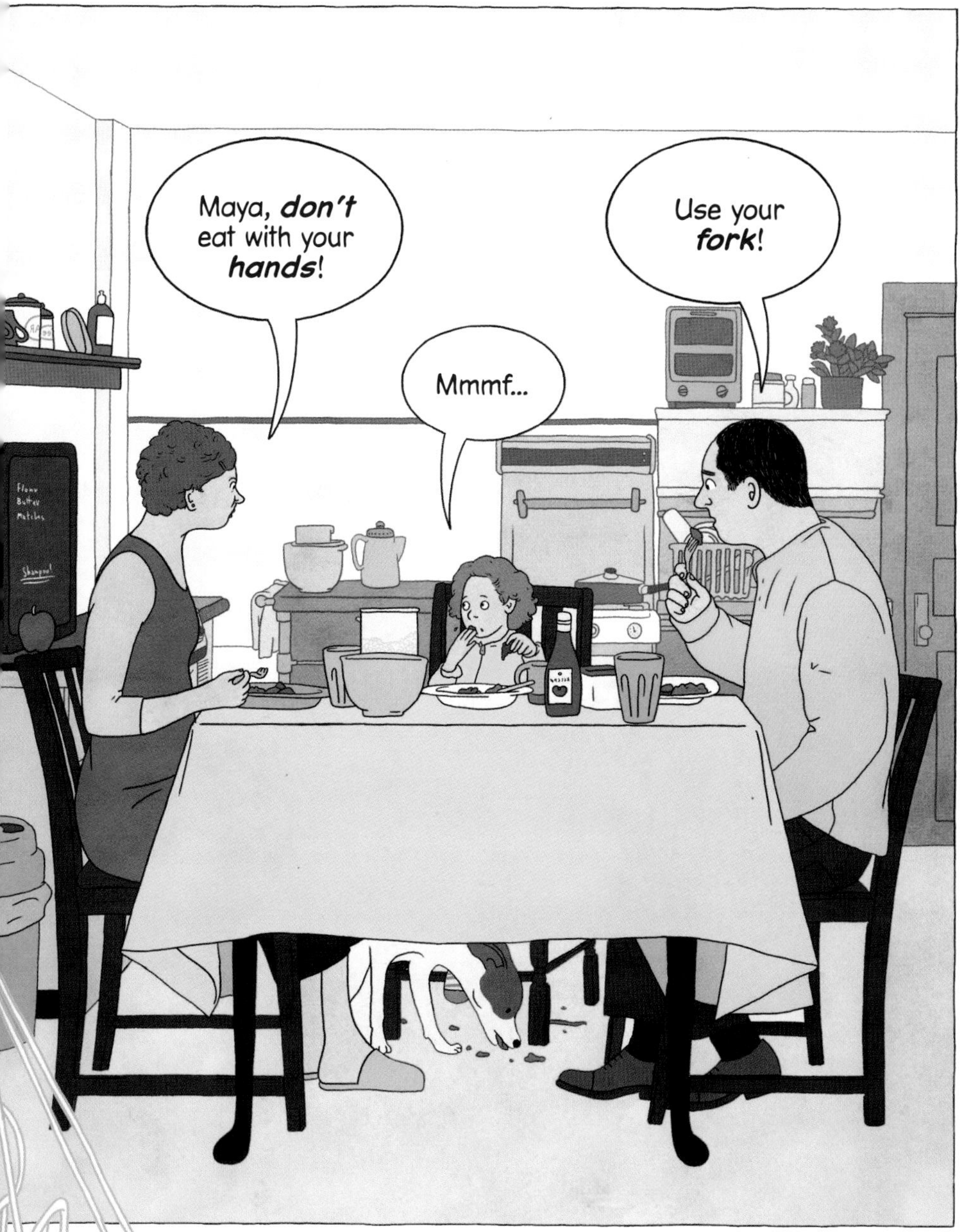
Maya, **don't** eat with your **hands**!
Mmmf...
Use your **fork**!

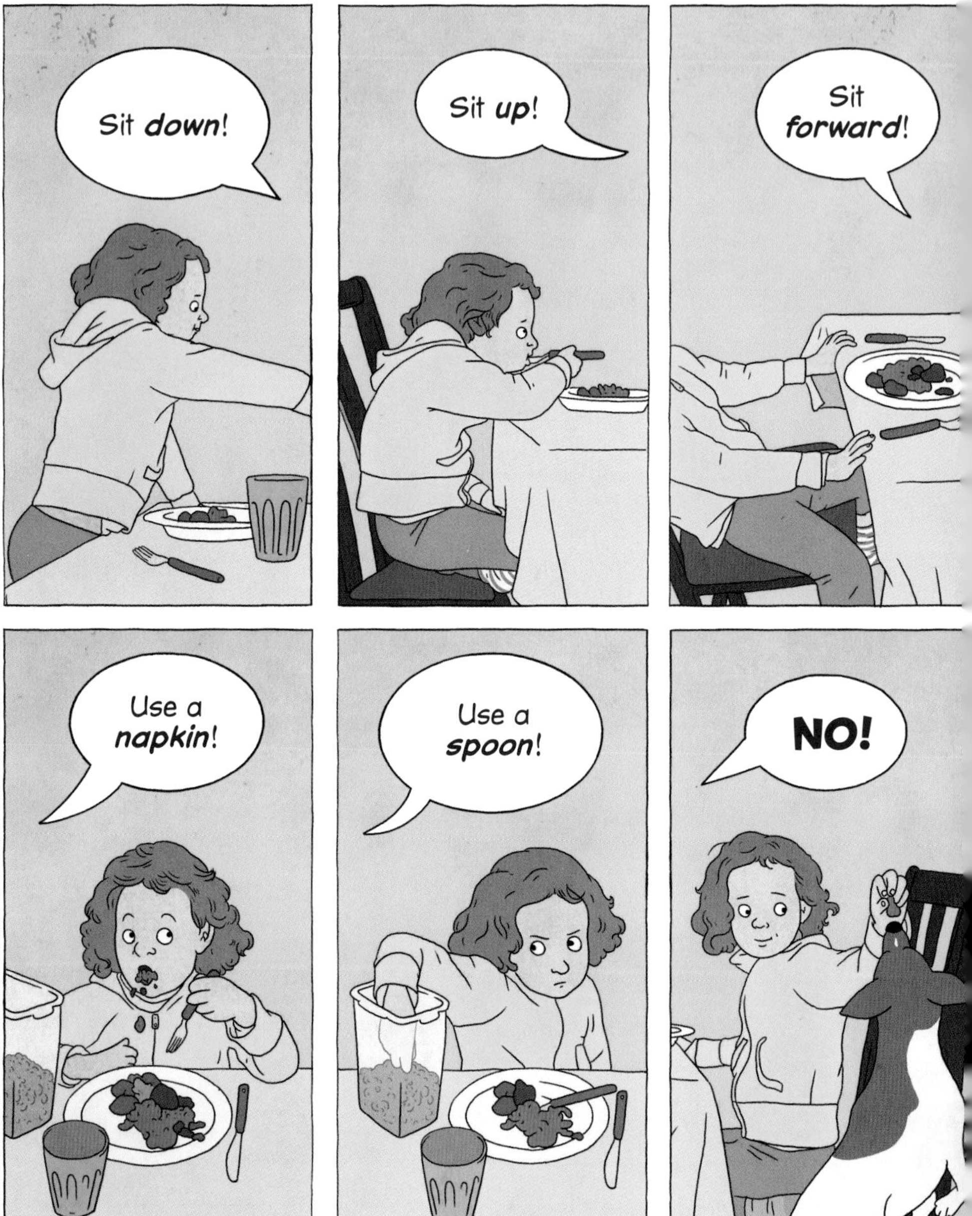
Sit **down**!
Sit **up**!
Sit **forward**!
Use a **napkin**!
Use a **spoon**!
NO!

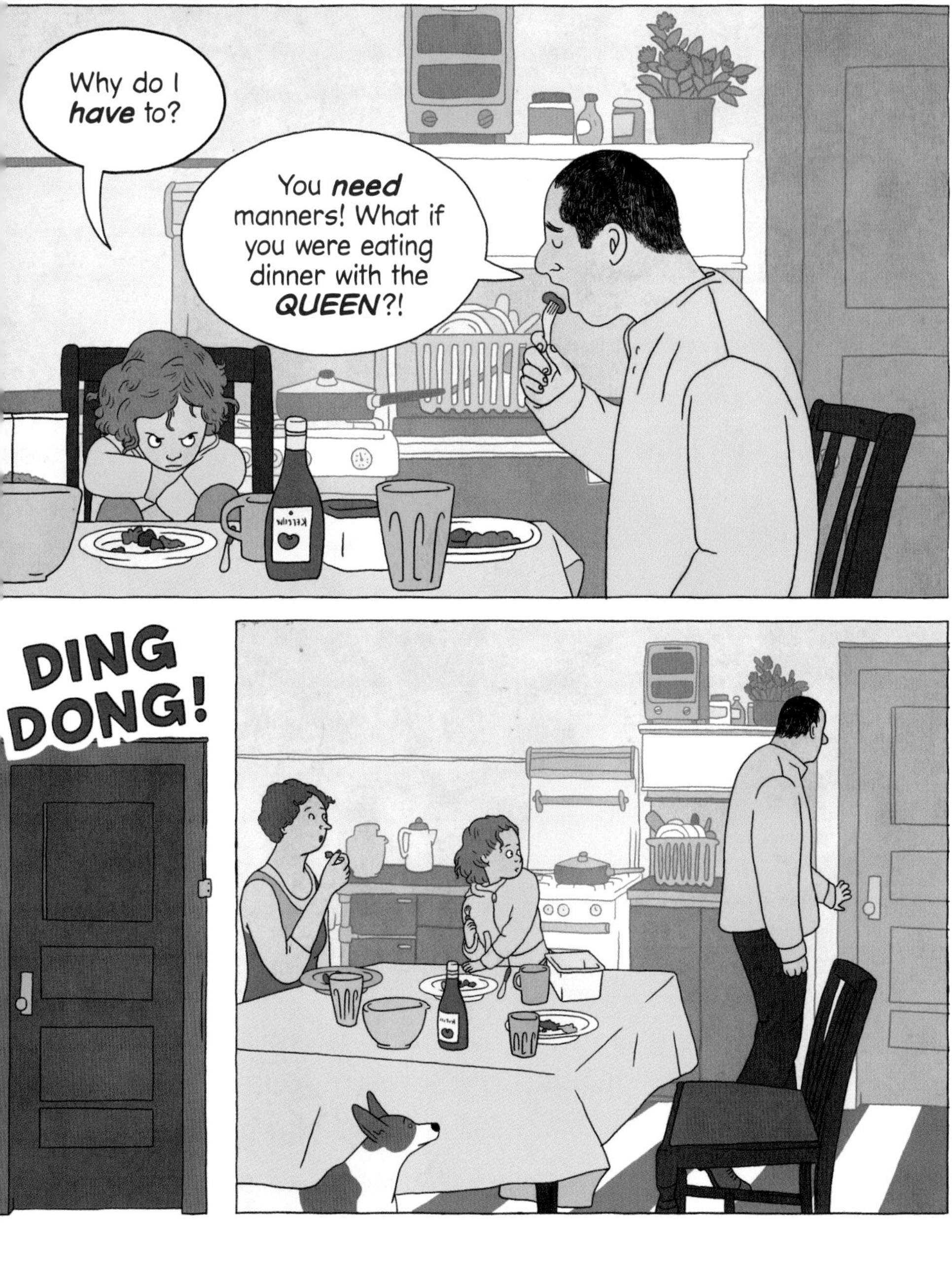
Why do I **have** to?
You **need** manners! What if you were eating dinner with the **QUEEN**?!
DING DONG!

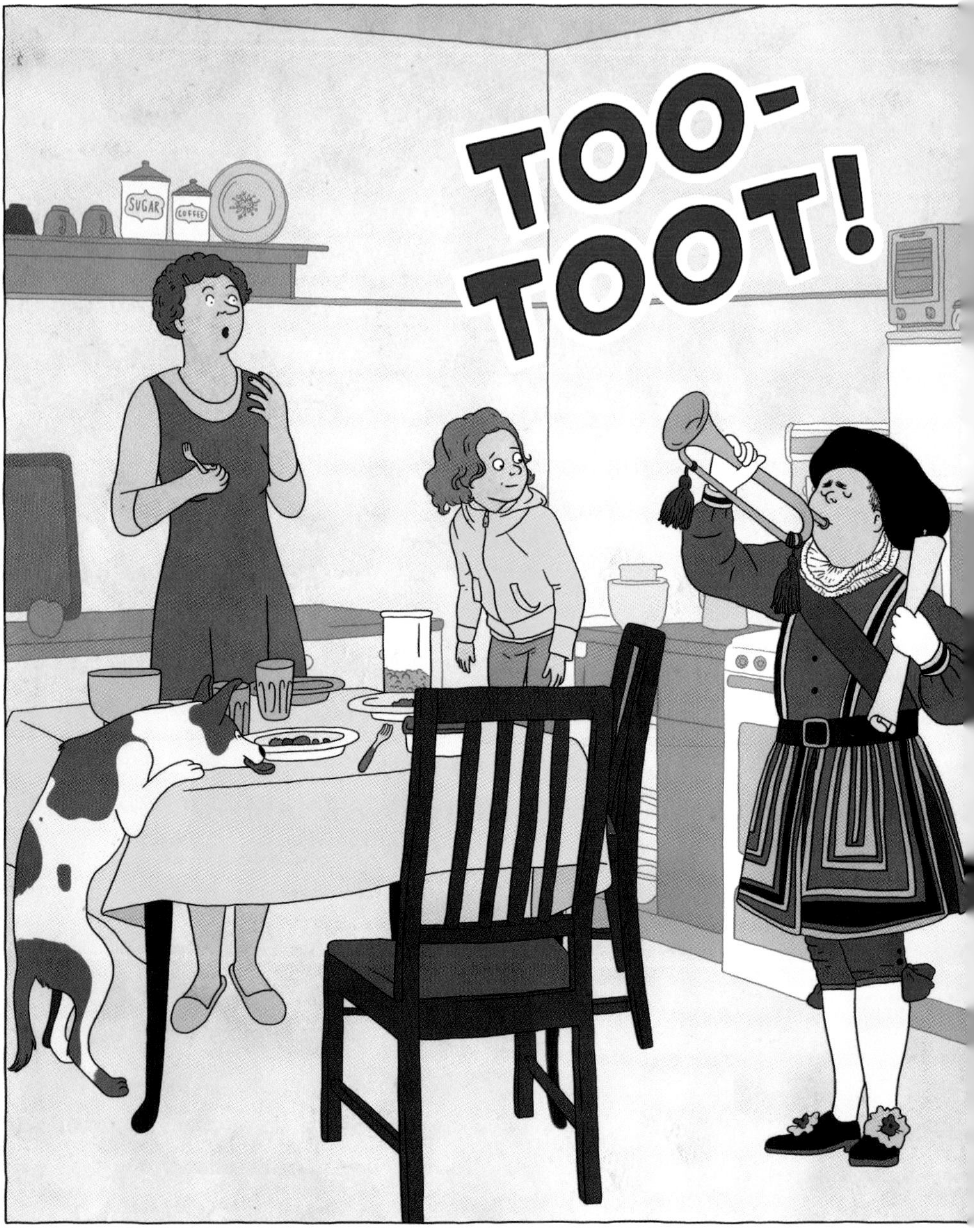
TOO-TOOT!
SUGAR
COFFEE

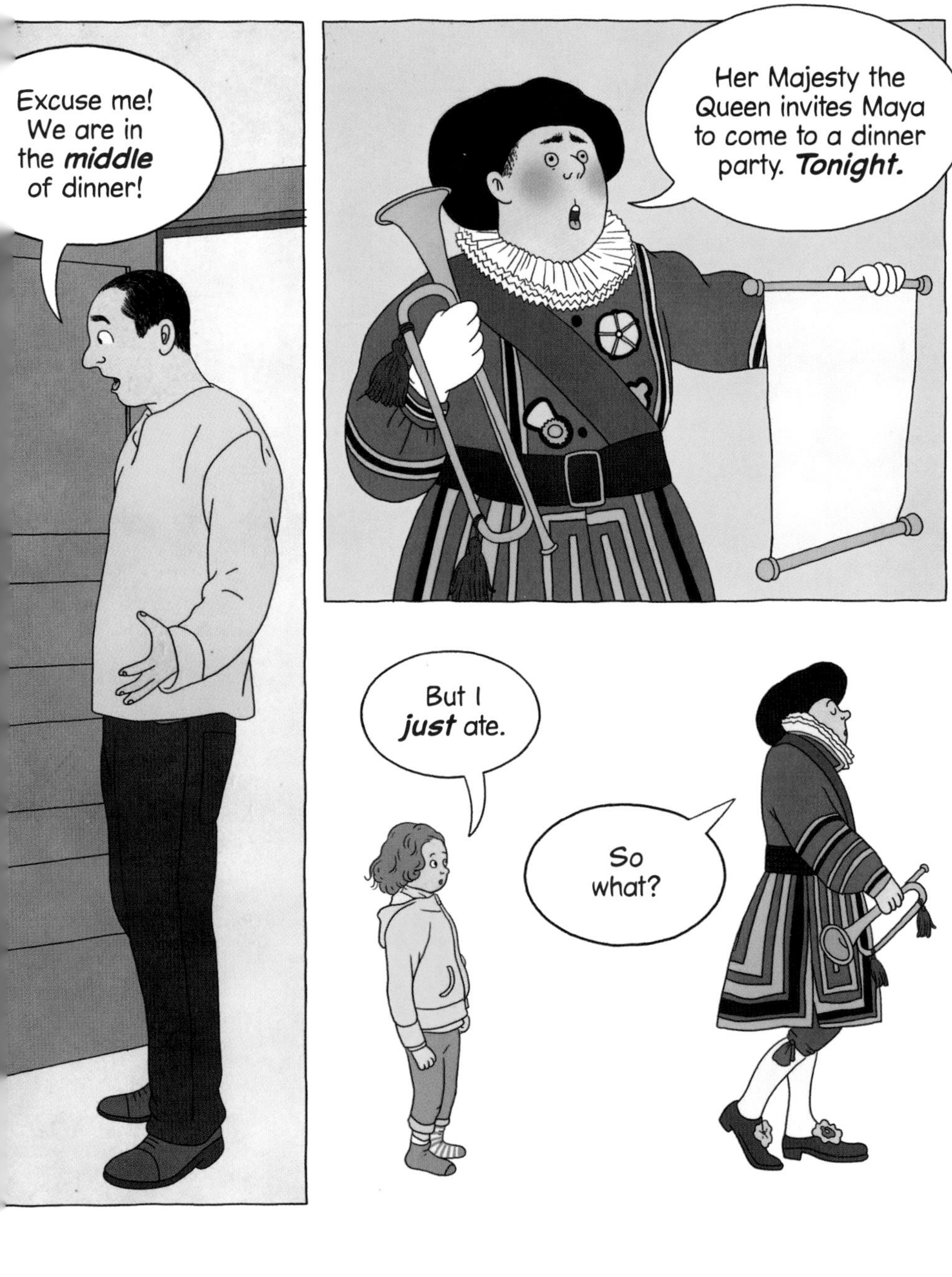
Excuse me! We are in the *middle* of dinner!
Her Majesty the Queen invites Maya to come to a dinner party. ***Tonight.***
But I *just* ate.
So what?

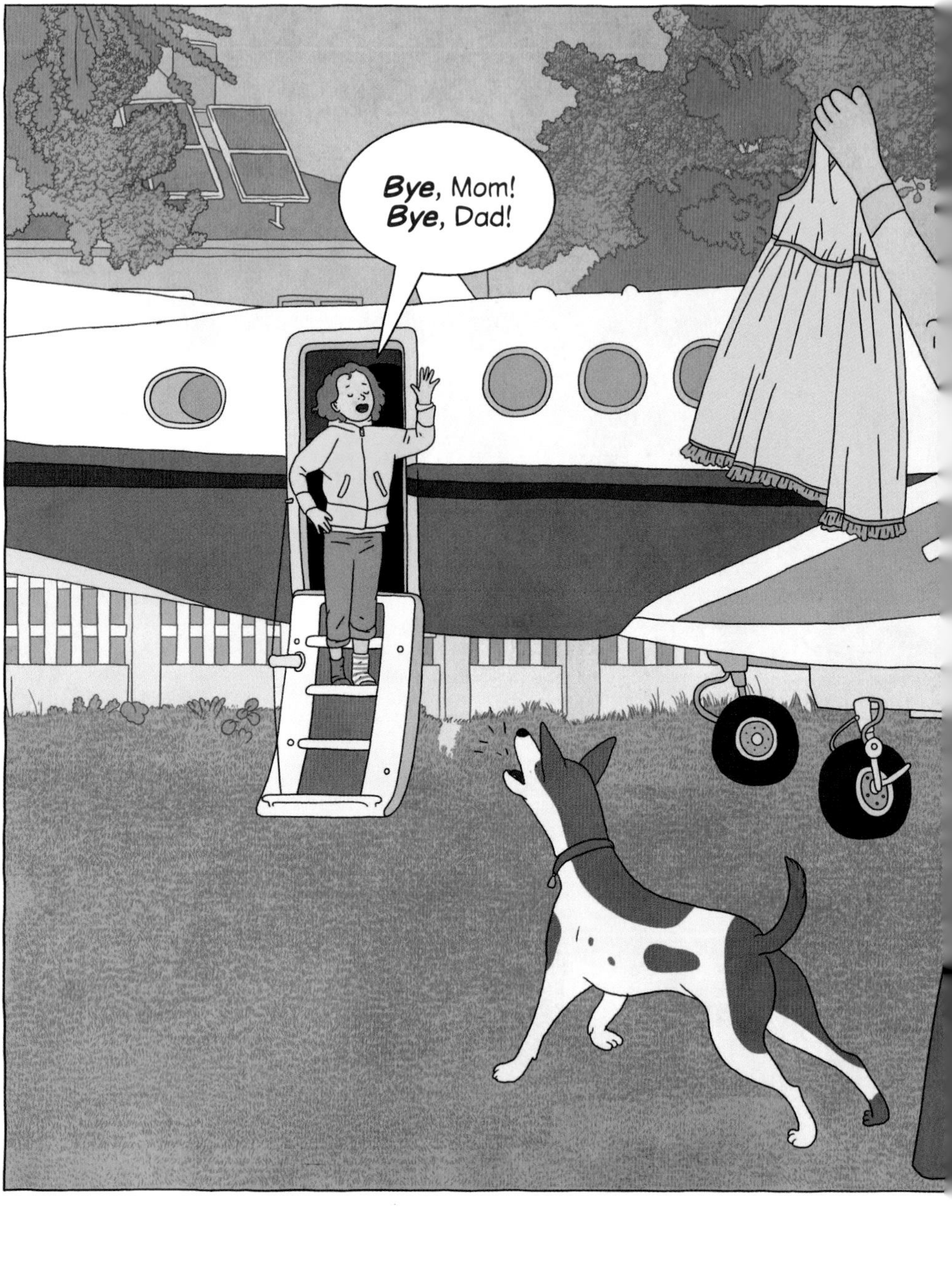
Bye, Mom! **Bye**, Dad!

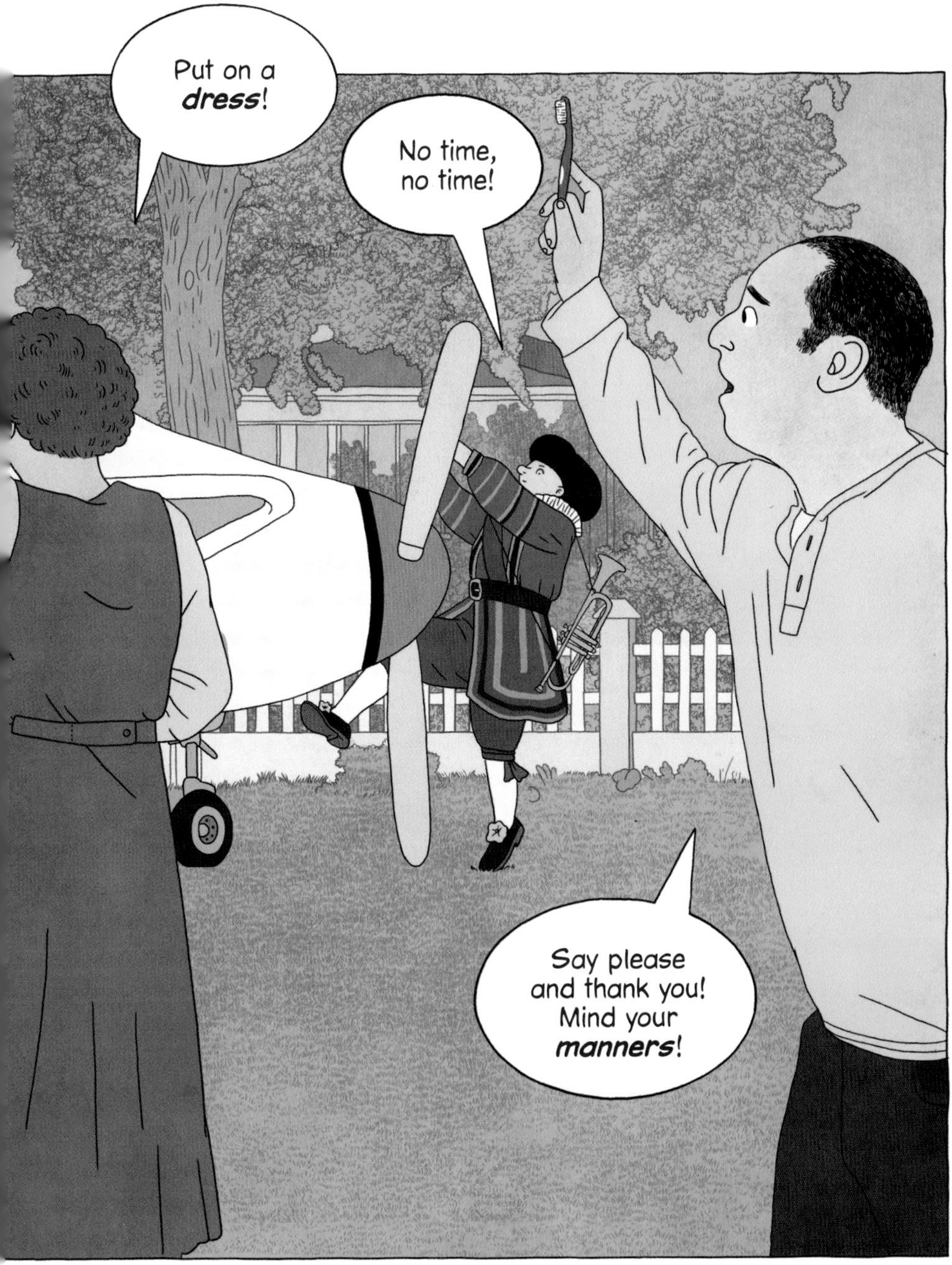
Put on a ***dress***!
No time, no time!
Say please and thank you! Mind your ***manners***!

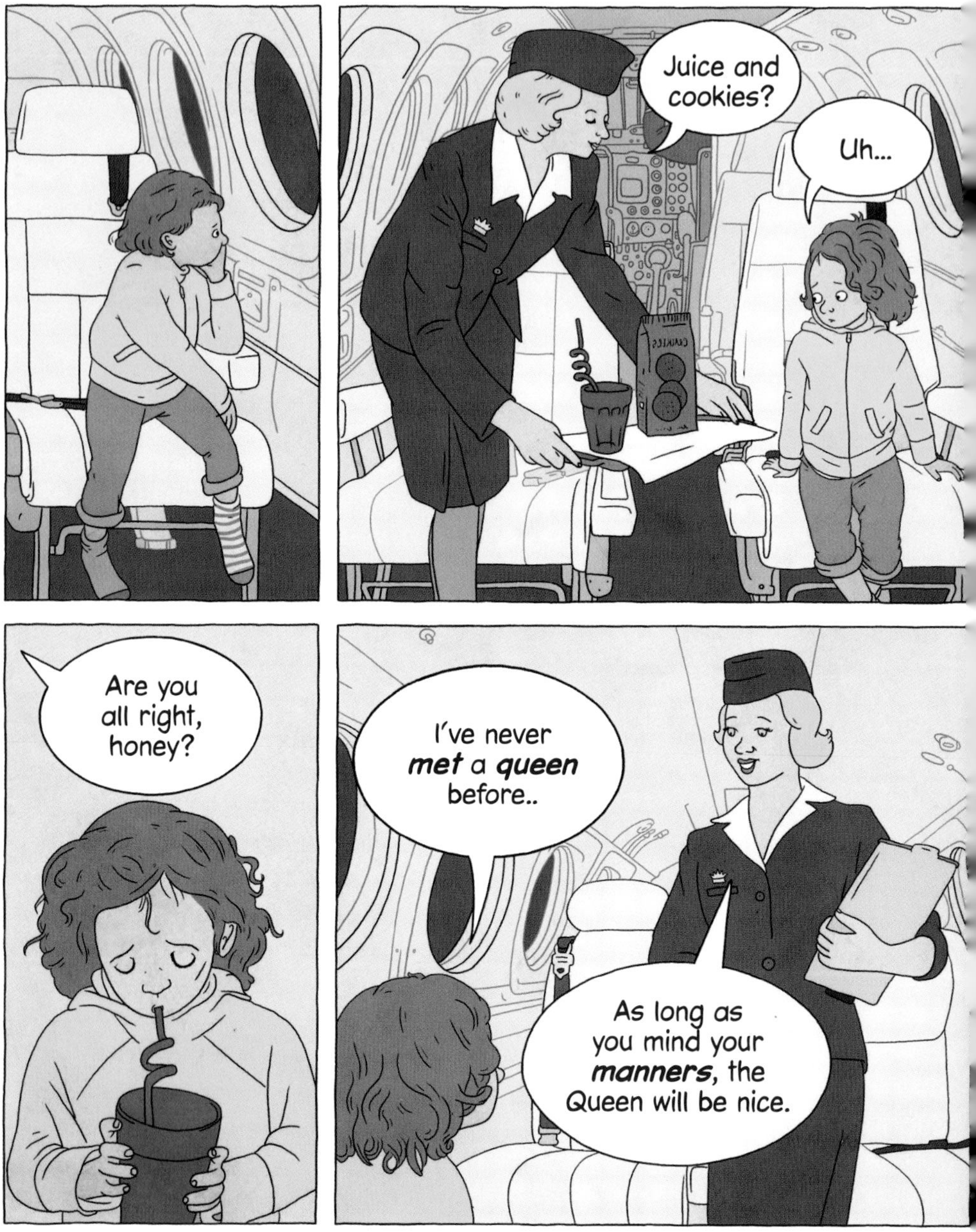
Juice and cookies?
Uh...
Are you all right, honey?
I've never ***met*** a ***queen*** before..
As long as you mind your ***manners,*** the Queen will be nice.

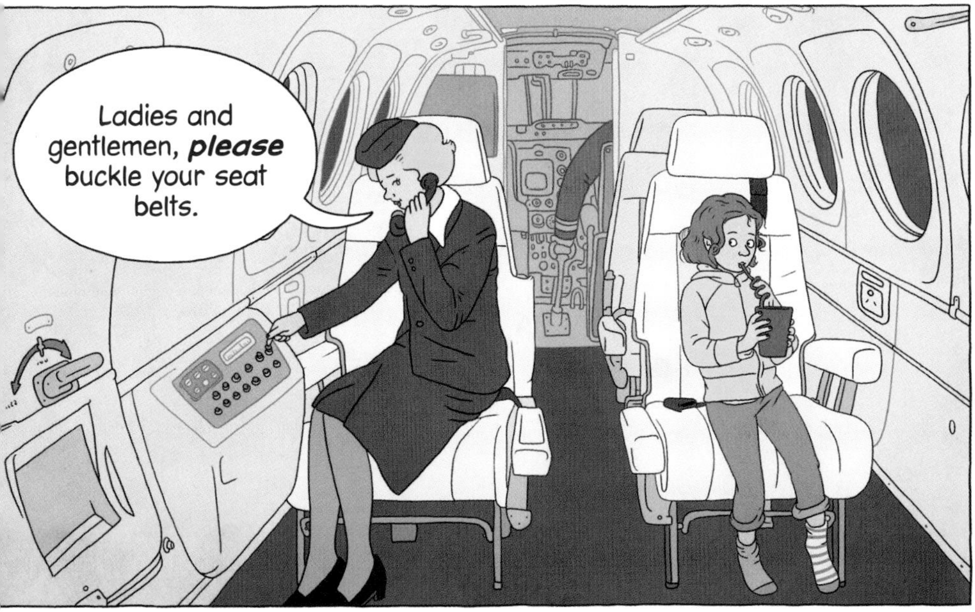
Ladies and gentlemen, ***please*** buckle your seat belts.

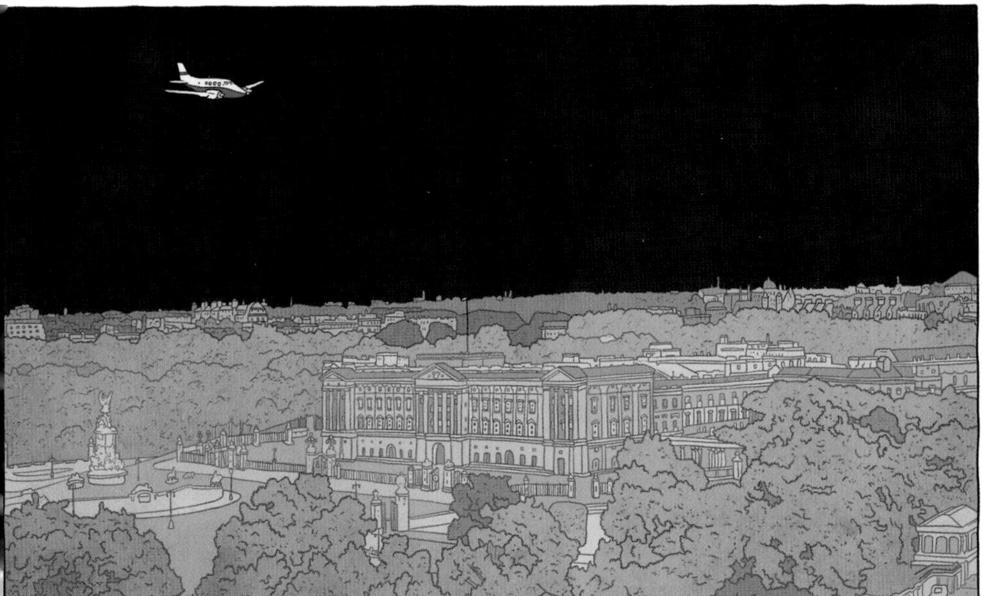

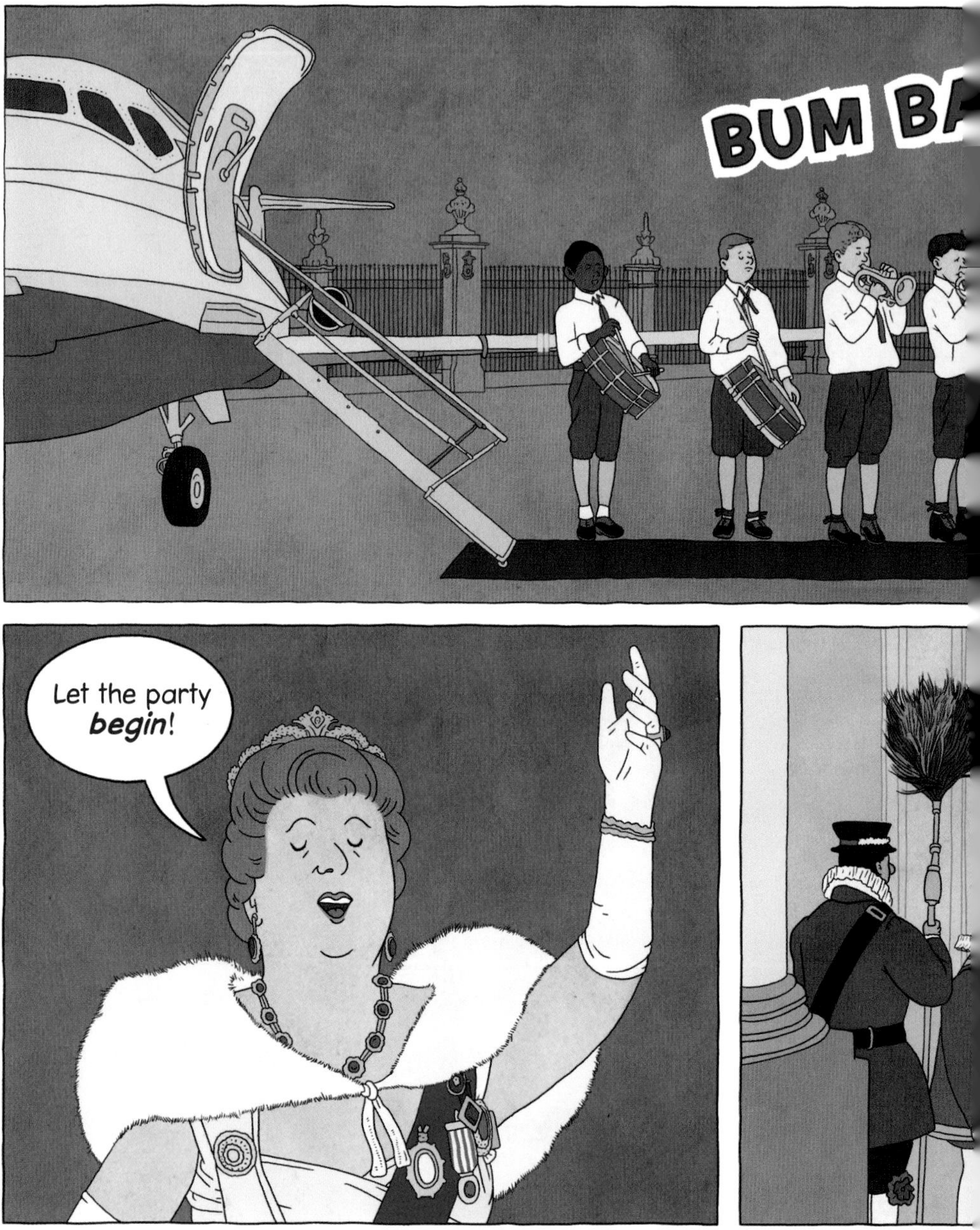
BUM BA
Let the party *begin*!

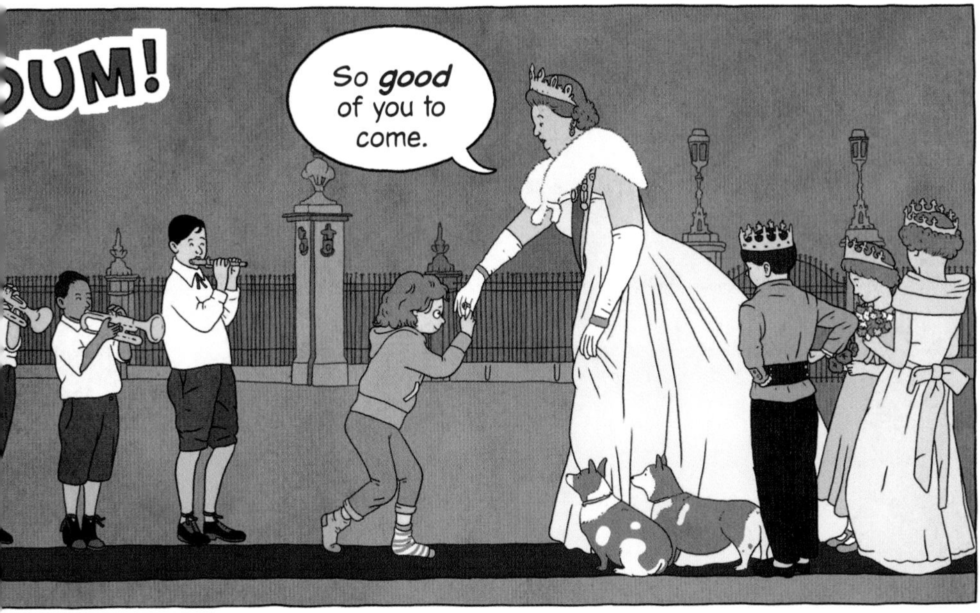

OUM!
So *good* of you to come.

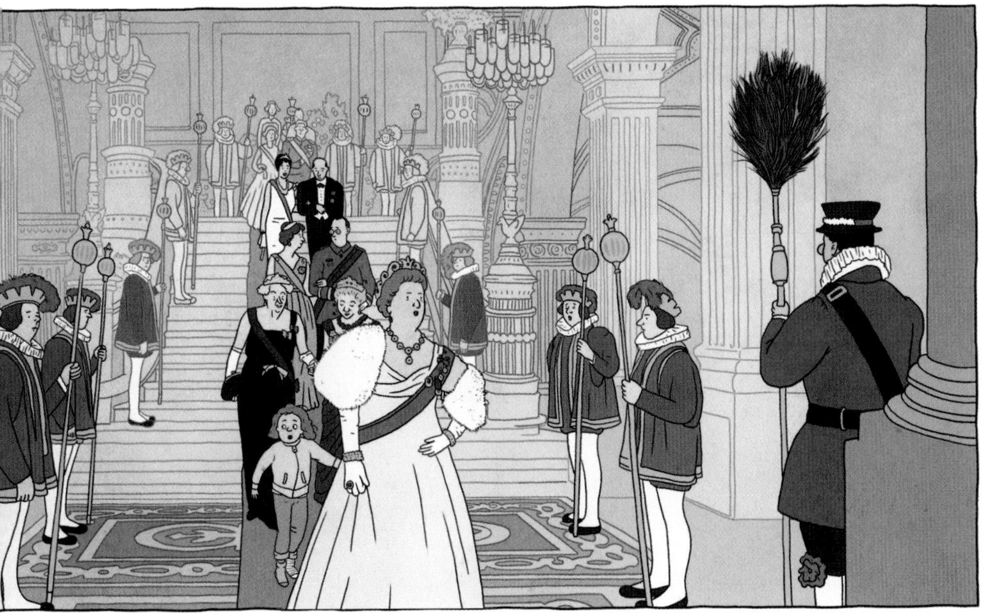

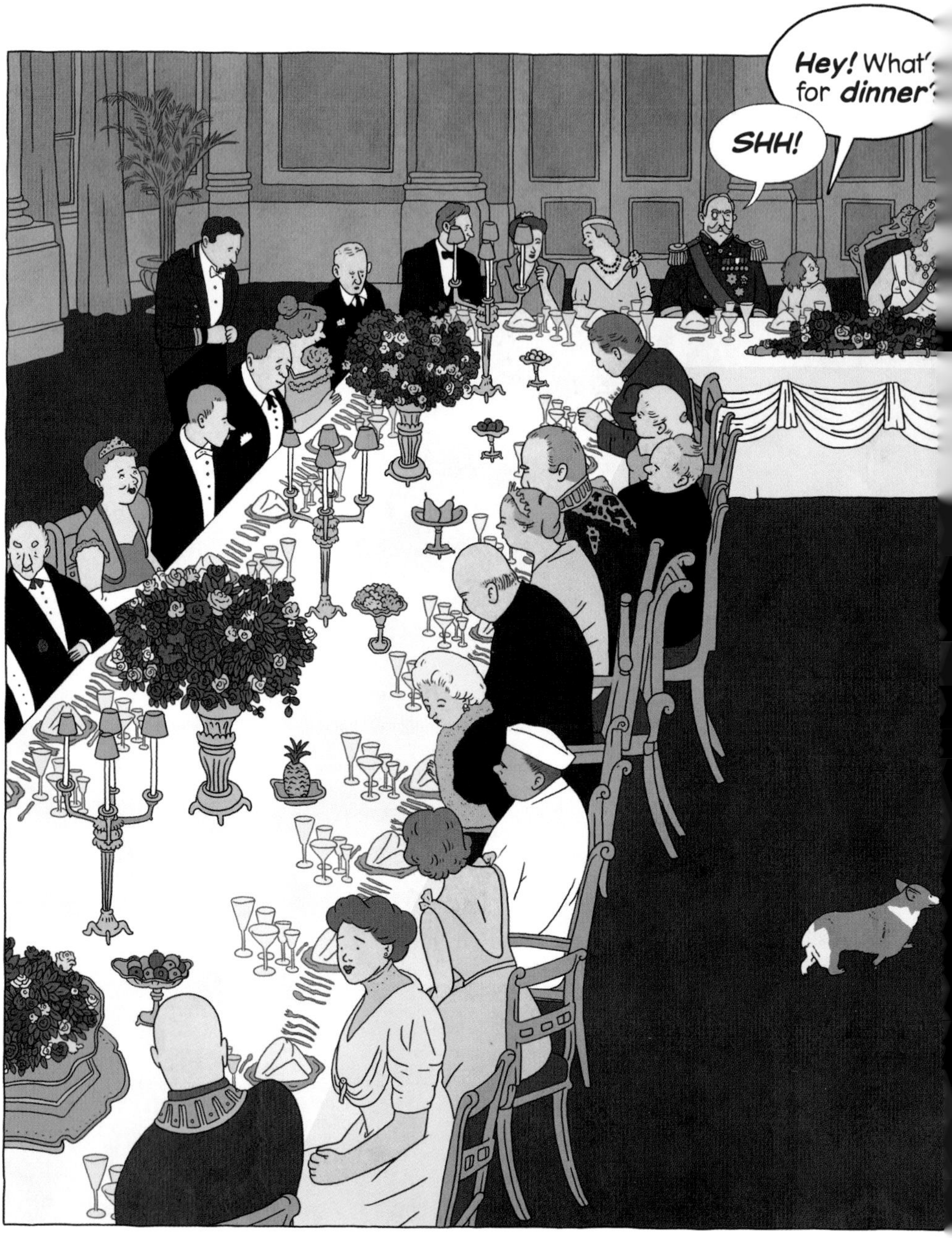
Hey! What's
for dinner?
SHH!

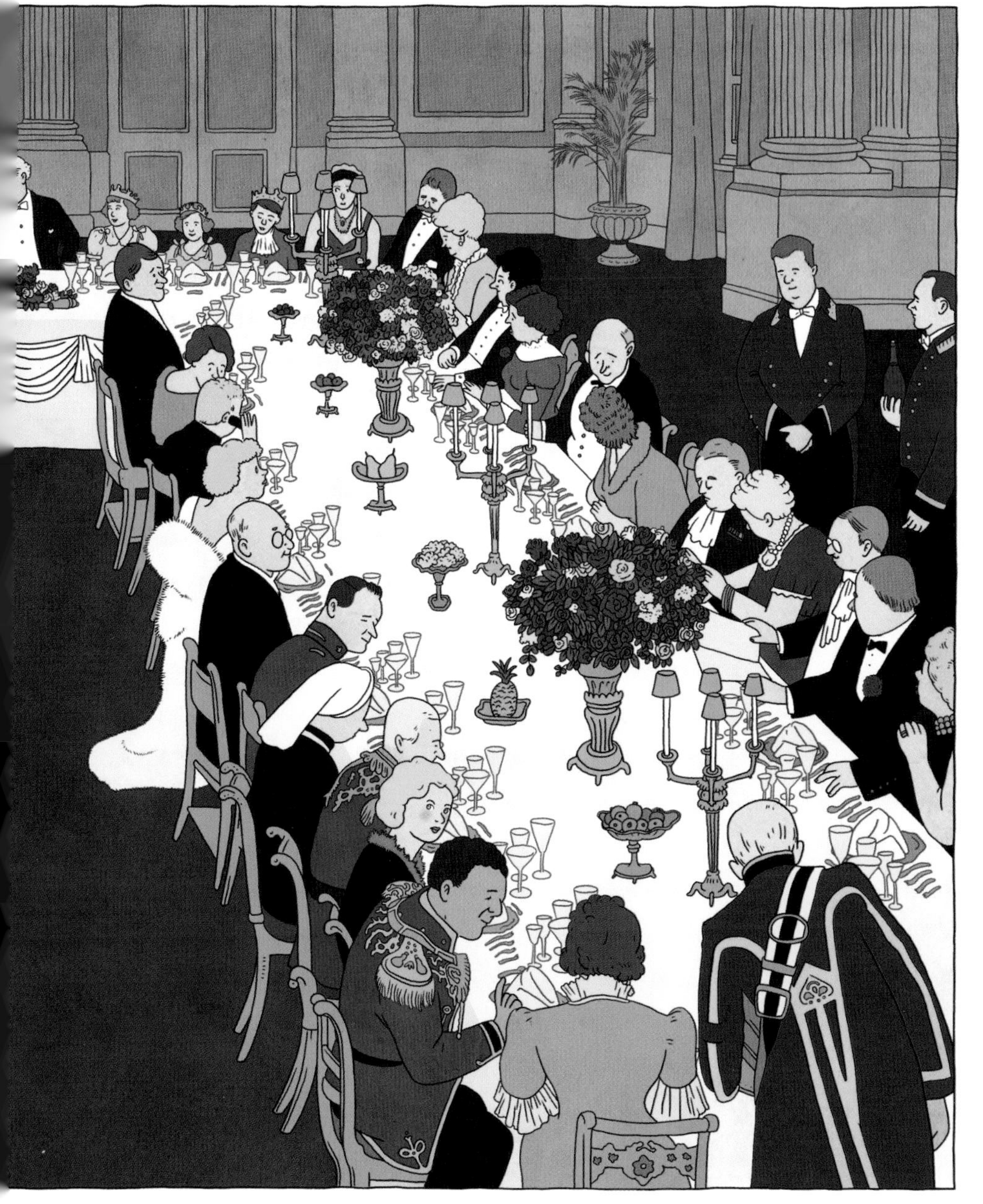

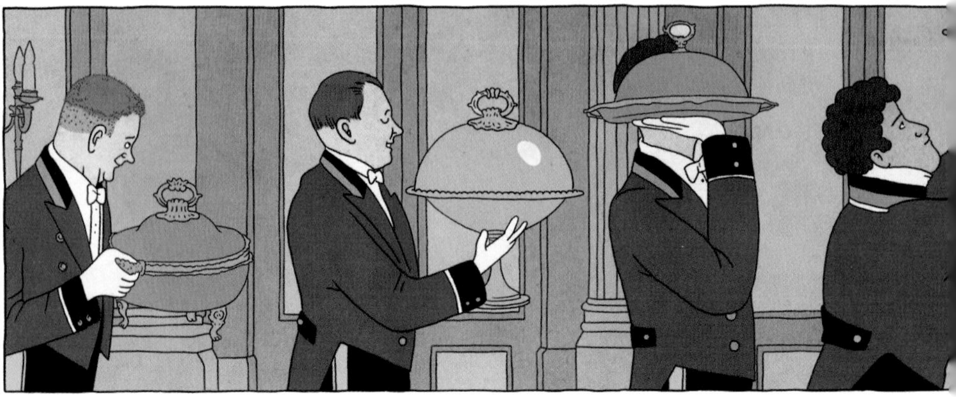

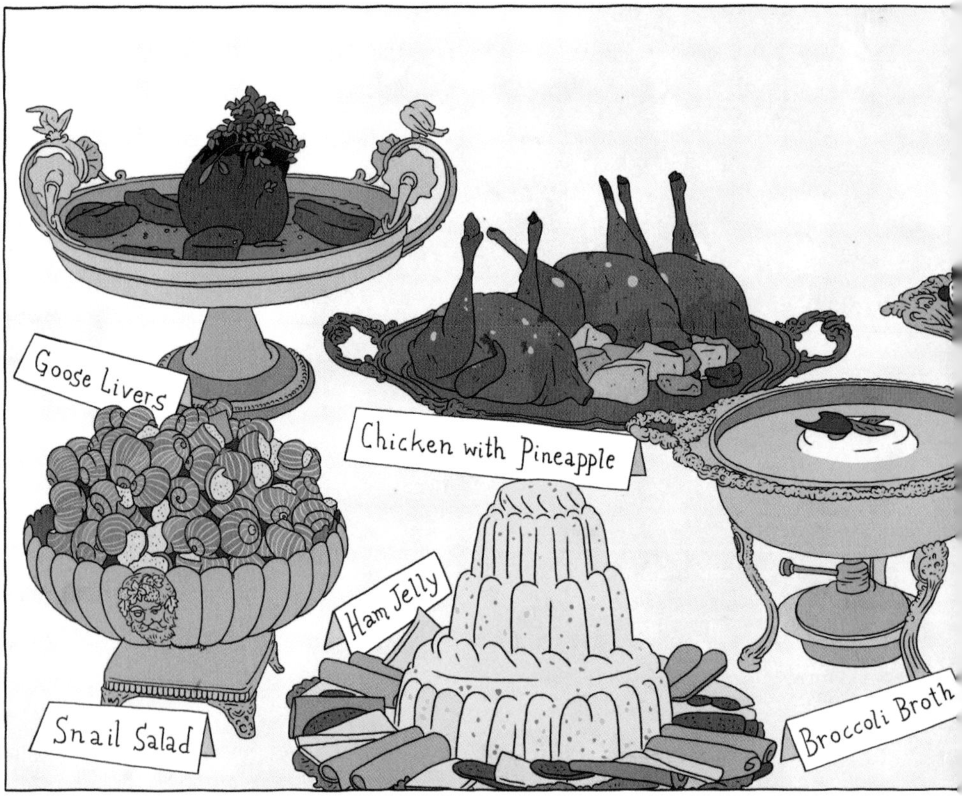
Goose Livers
Chicken with Pineapple
Ham Jelly
Snail Salad
Broccoli Broth

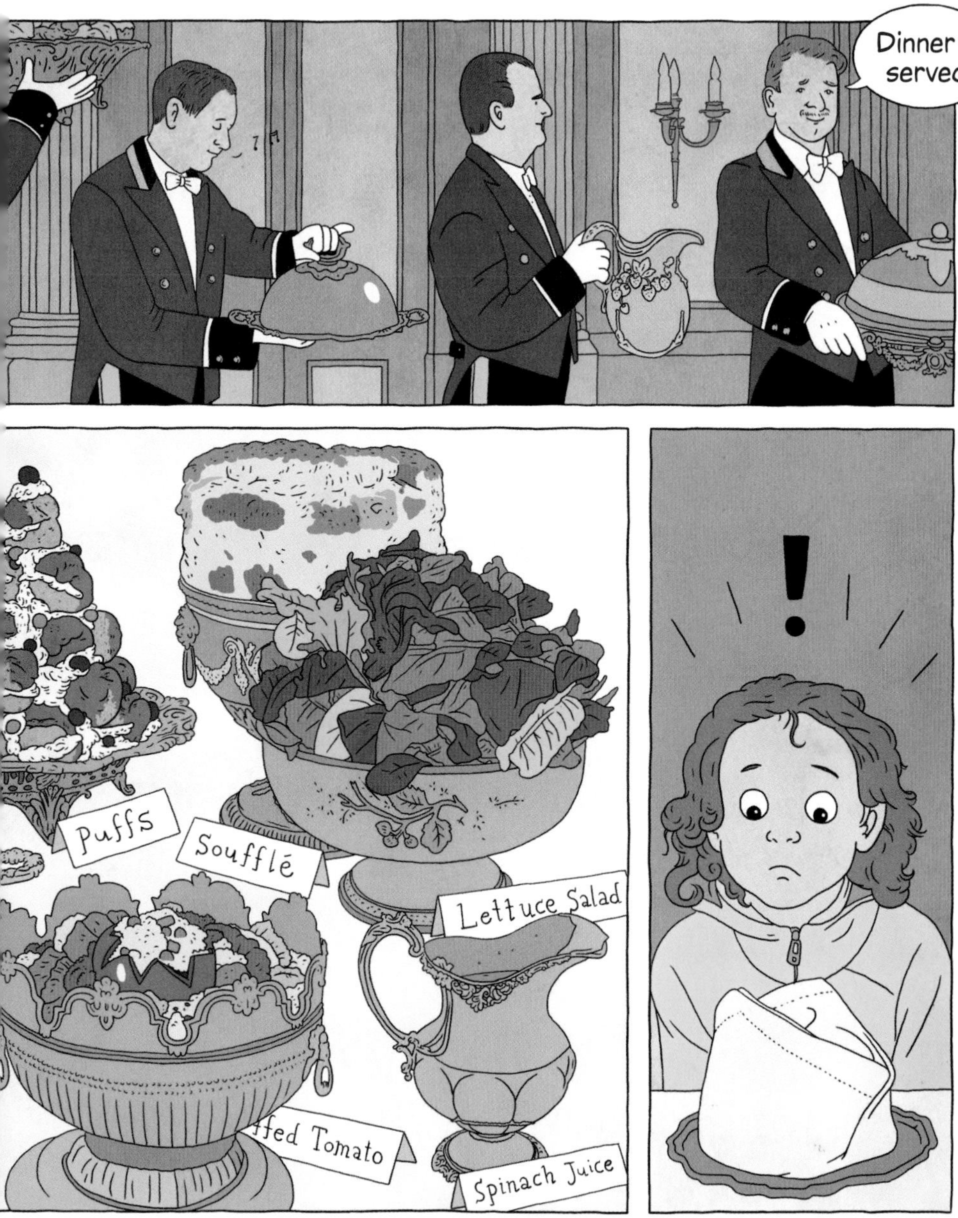

Dinner is served!
Puffs
Soufflé
Lettuce Salad
ffed Tomato
Spinach Juice
!

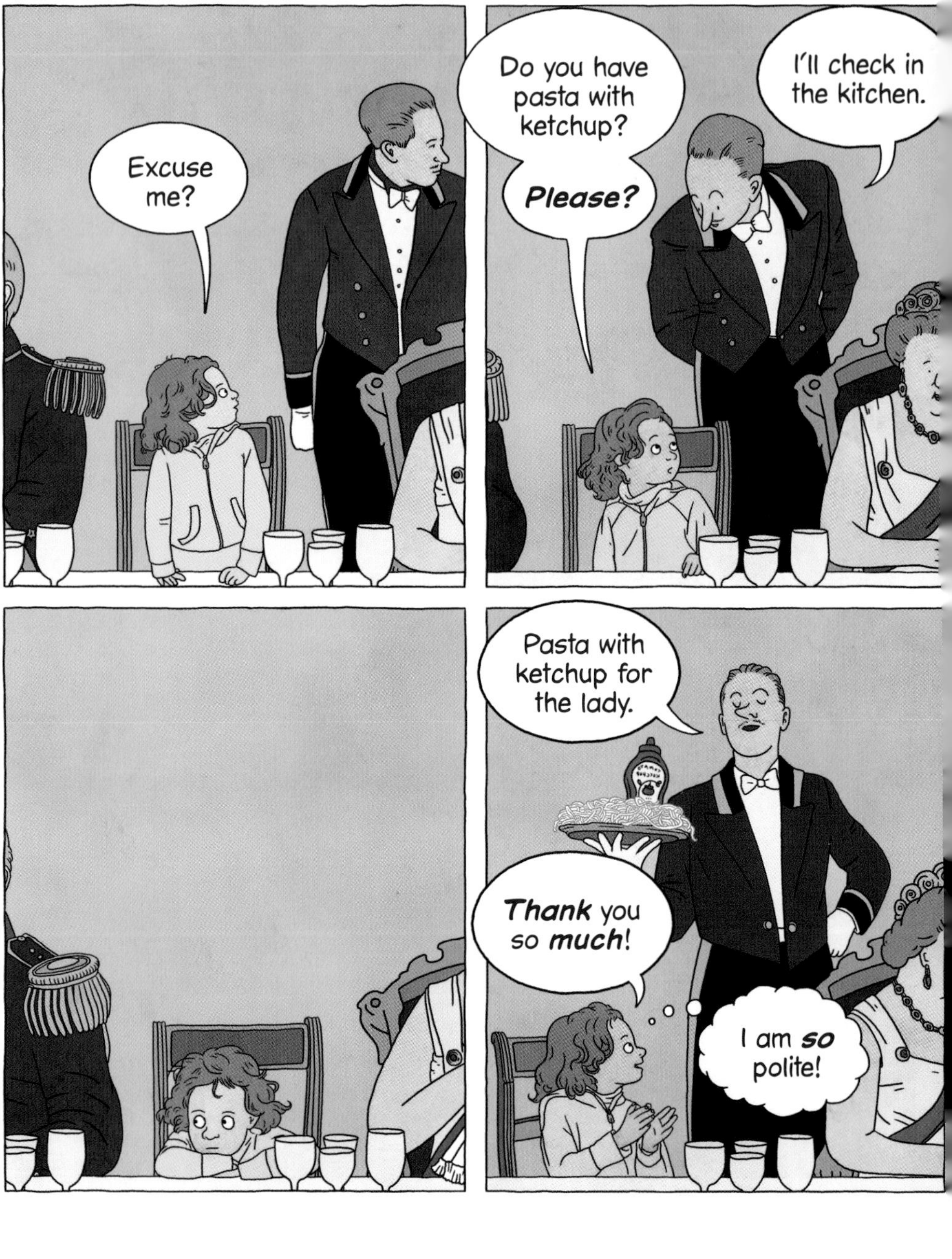
Excuse me?
Do you have pasta with ketchup?
Please?
I'll check in the kitchen.
Pasta with ketchup for the lady.
Thank you so much!
I am so polite!

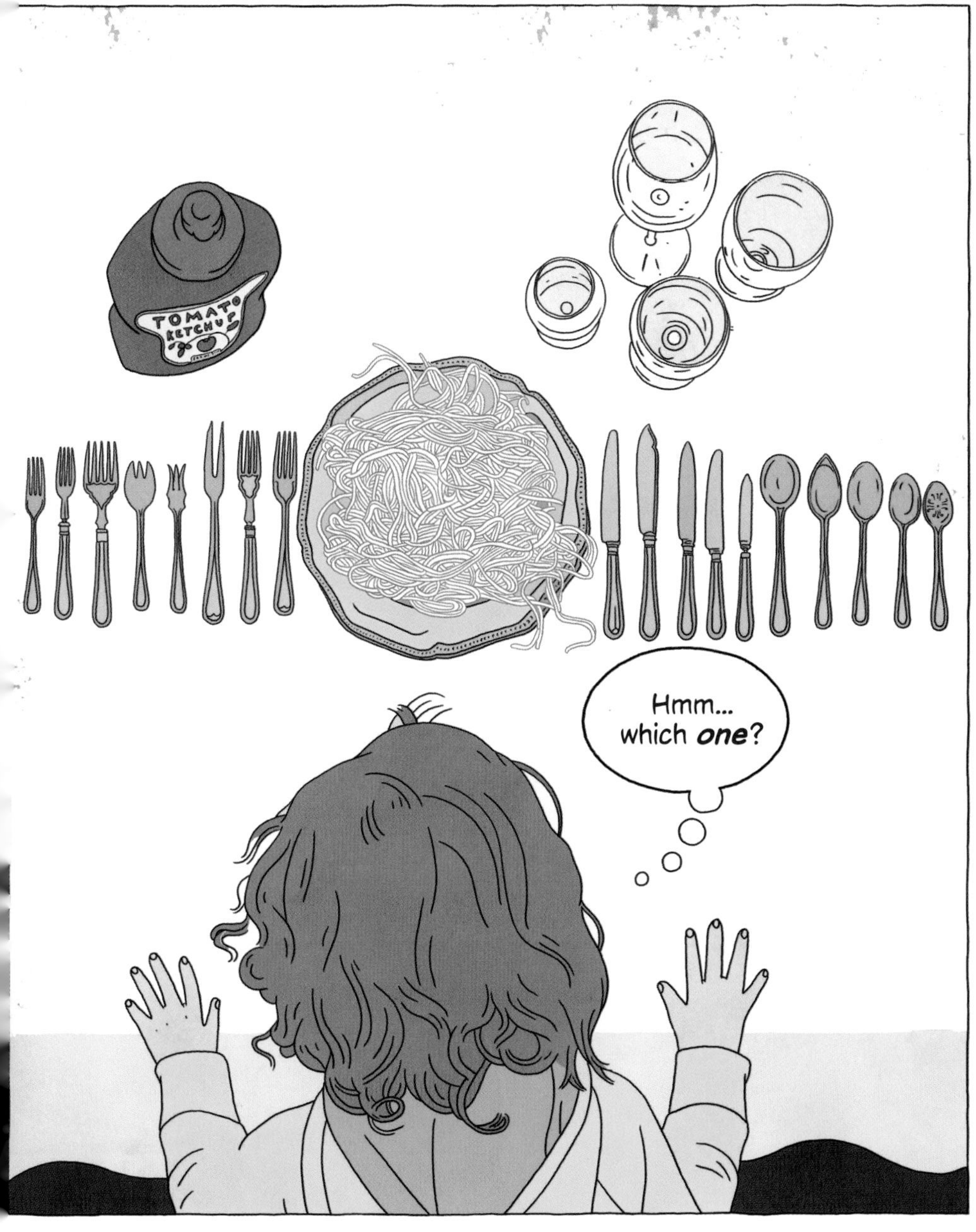
TOMATO KETCHUP
Hmm... which *one*?

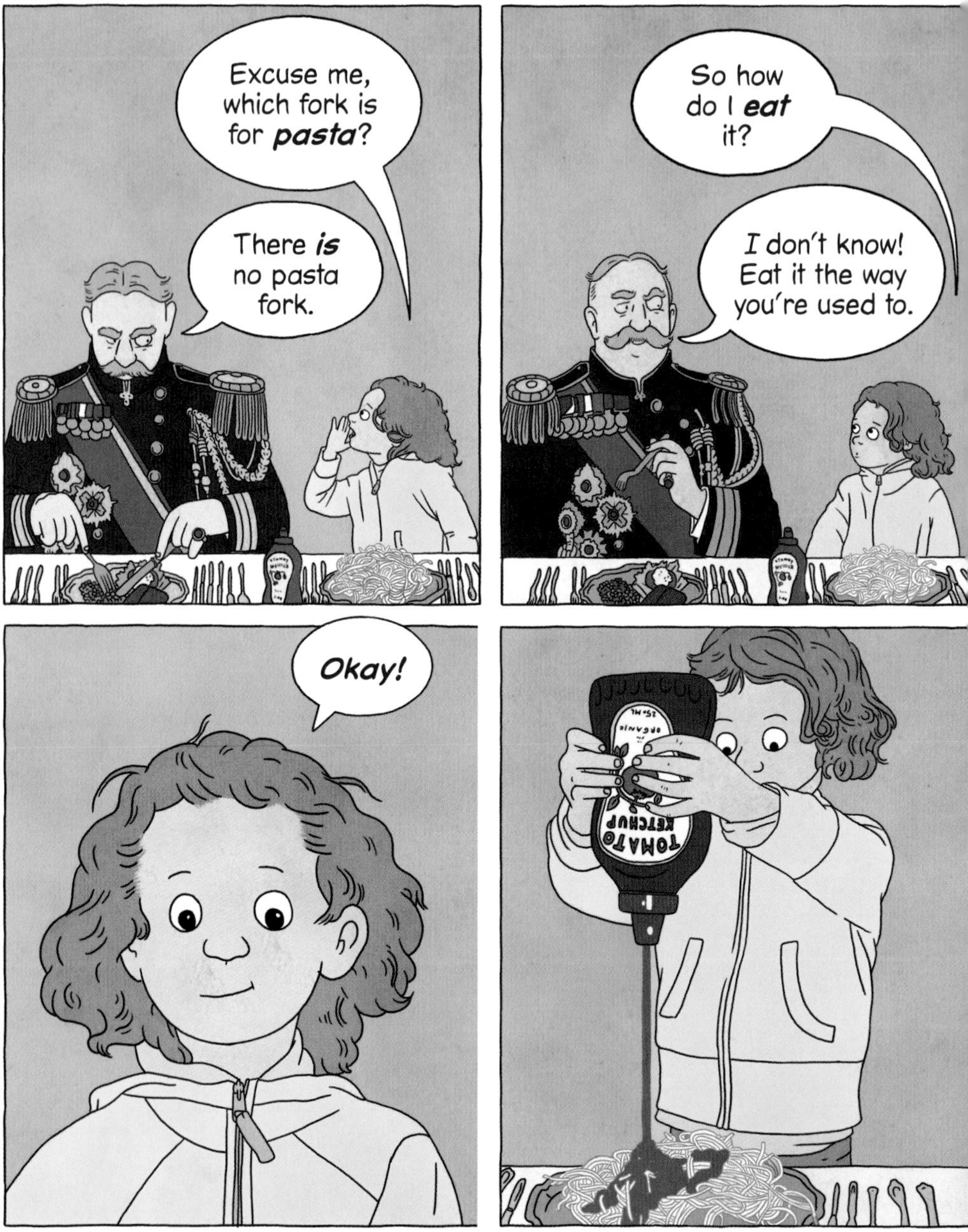
Excuse me, which fork is for ***pasta***?
There ***is*** no pasta fork.
So how do I ***eat*** it?
I don't know! Eat it the way you're used to.
Okay!
TOMATO KETCHUP

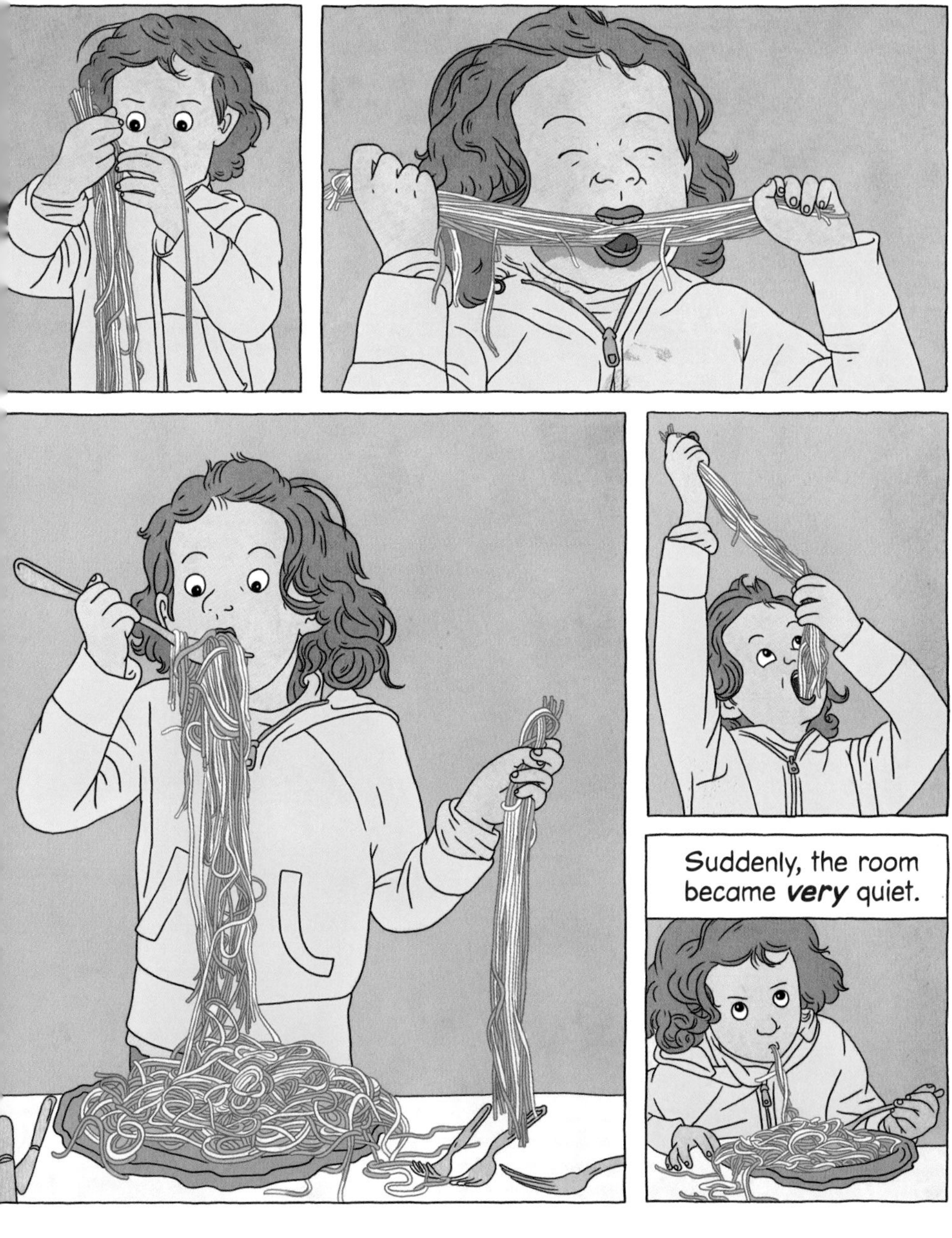
Suddenly, the room became *very* quiet.

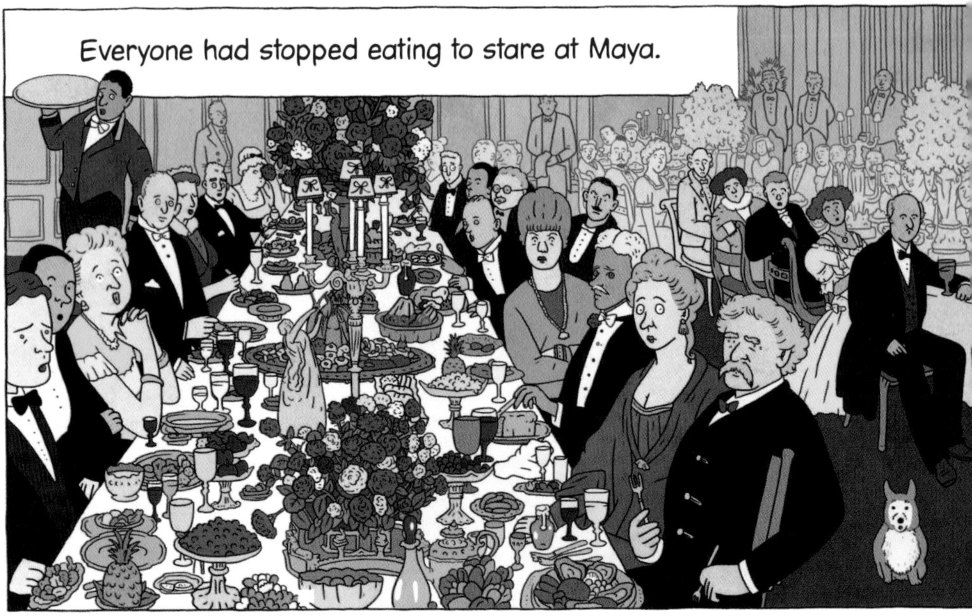
Everyone had stopped eating to stare at Maya.

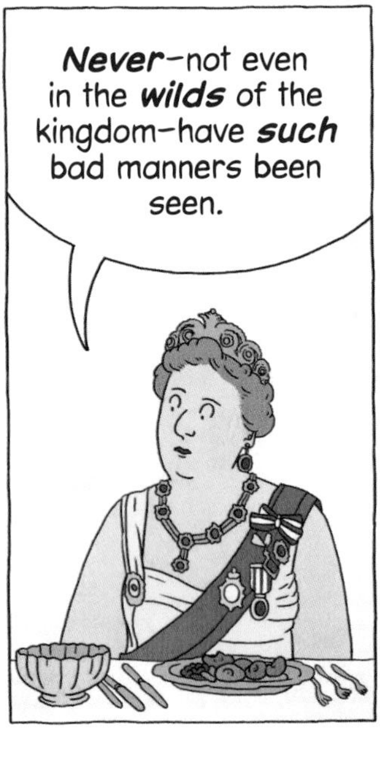
Never—not even in the ***wilds*** of the kingdom—have ***such*** bad manners been seen.

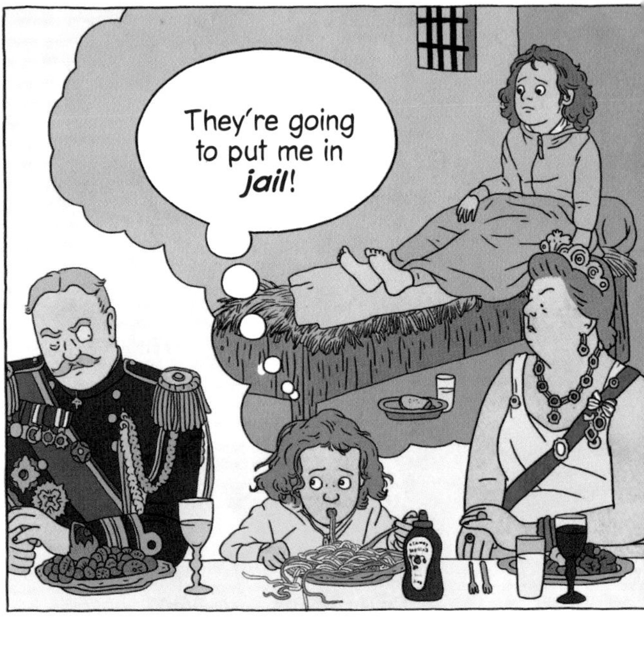
They're going to put me in ***jail***!

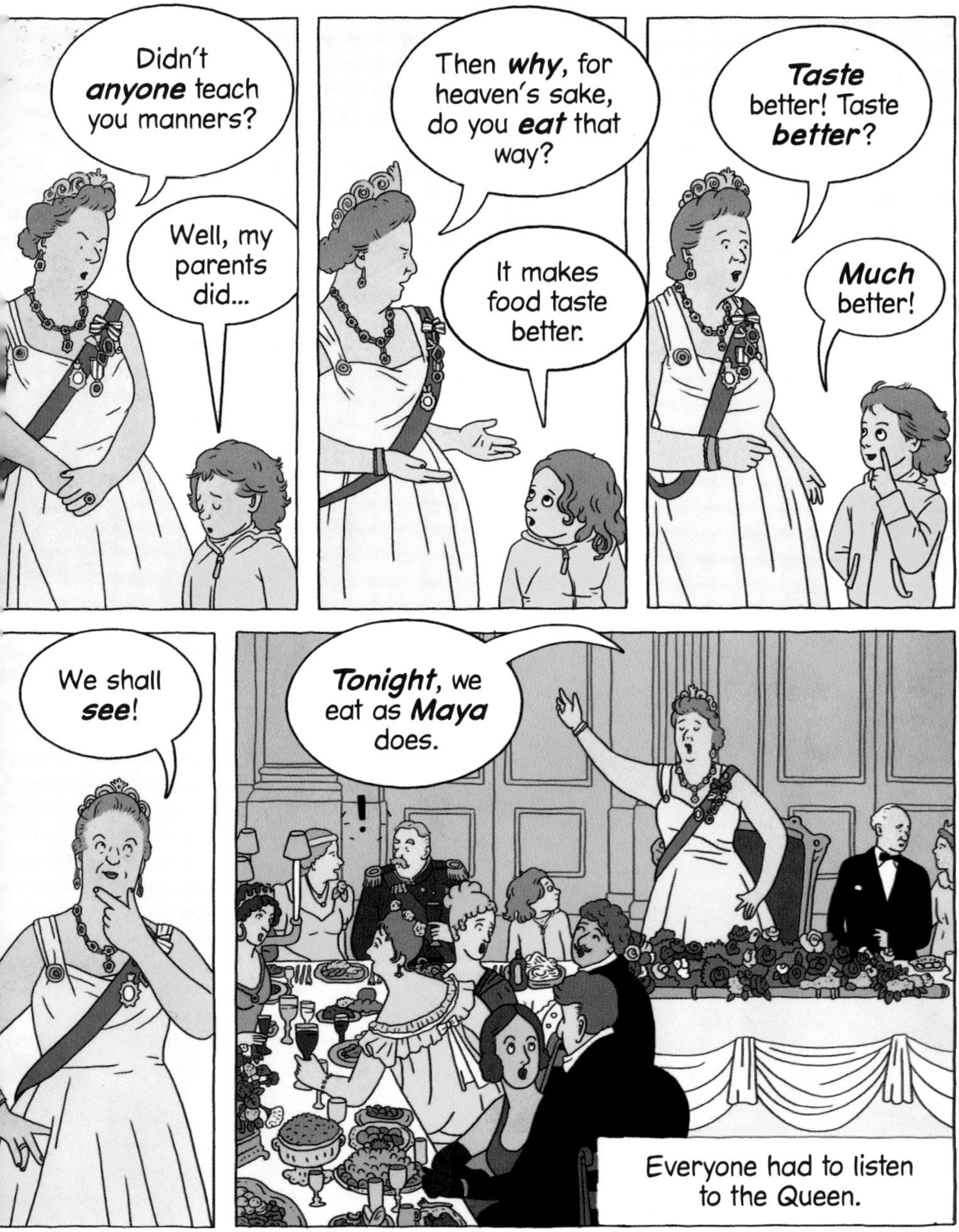

Didn't **anyone** teach you manners?
Well, my parents did...
Then **why**, for heaven's sake, do you **eat** that way?
It makes food taste better.
Taste better! Taste **better**?
Much better!
We shall **see**!
Tonight, we eat as **Maya** does.
!
Everyone had to listen to the Queen.

The Duke ate the chicken with his hands.
The Princess put her face in the soup bowl.
The Countess put her hands in the salad.
The Duchess fed cheese to the dog.

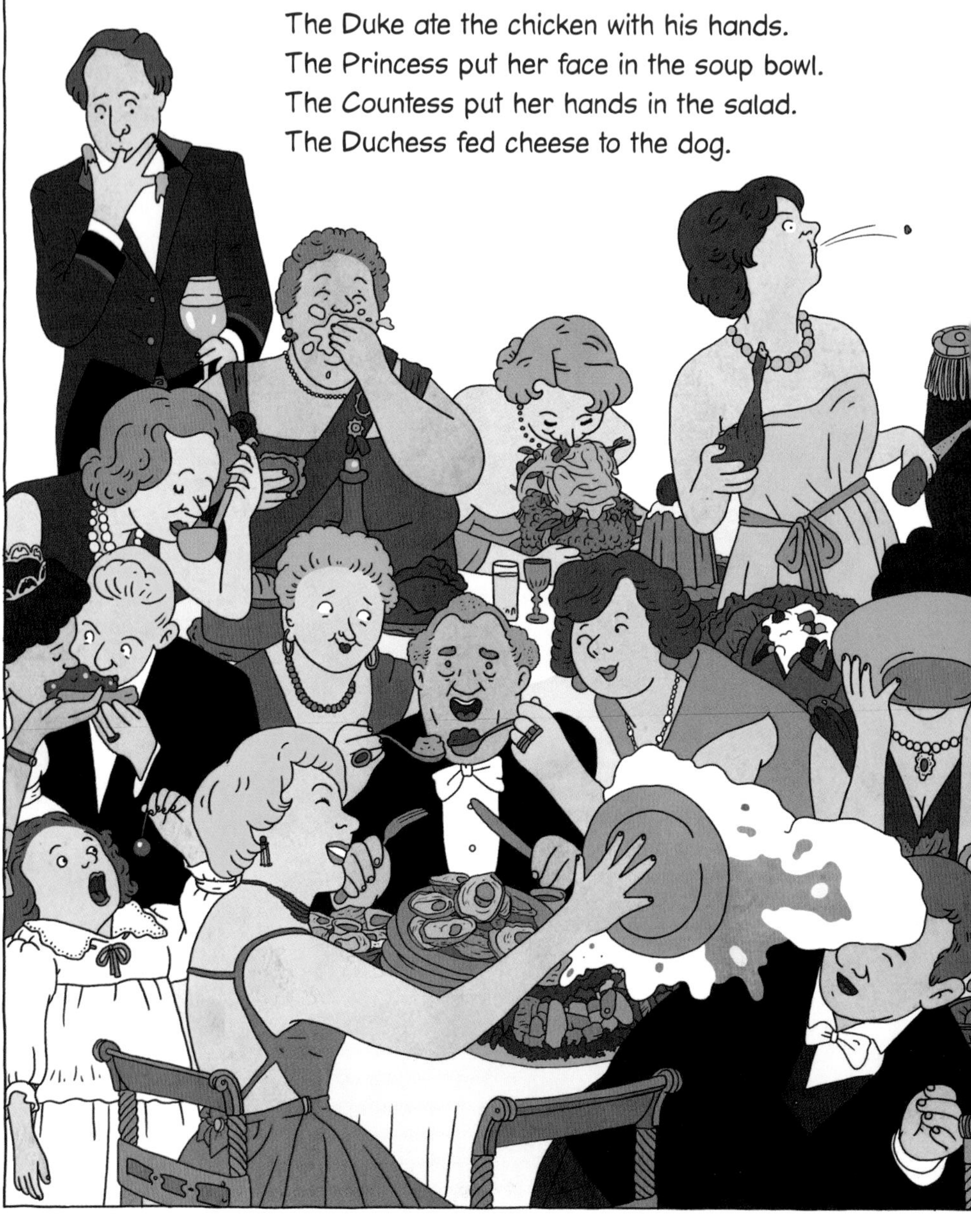

But the Queen outdid them all.

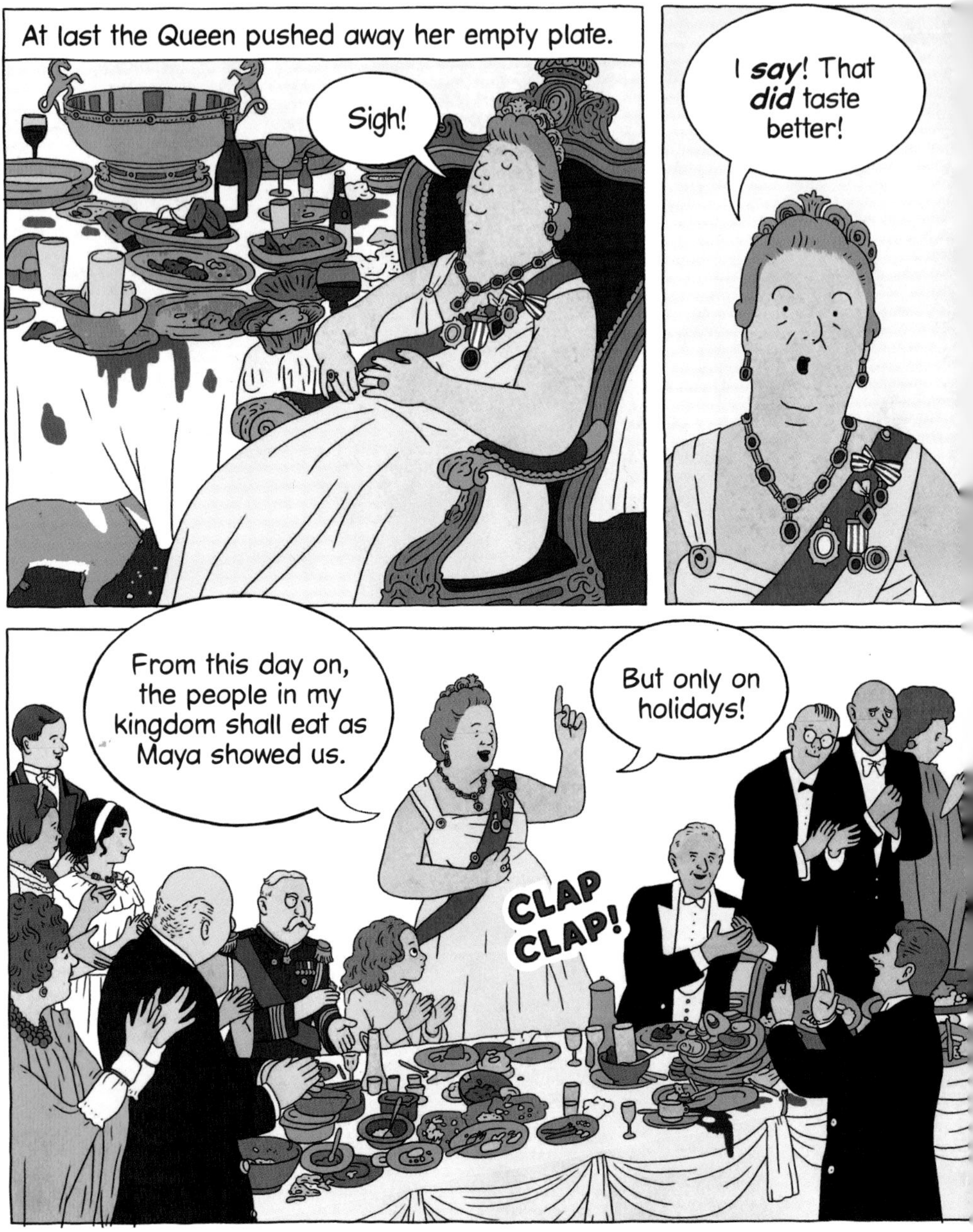
At last the Queen pushed away her empty plate.
Sigh!
I *say*! That *did* taste better!
From this day on, the people in my kingdom shall eat as Maya showed us.
But only on holidays!
CLAP CLAP!

How can our kingdom *ever* thank you?

Can I have dessert?

May the dessert be *served*!

Cooks came in with piles of ice cream.

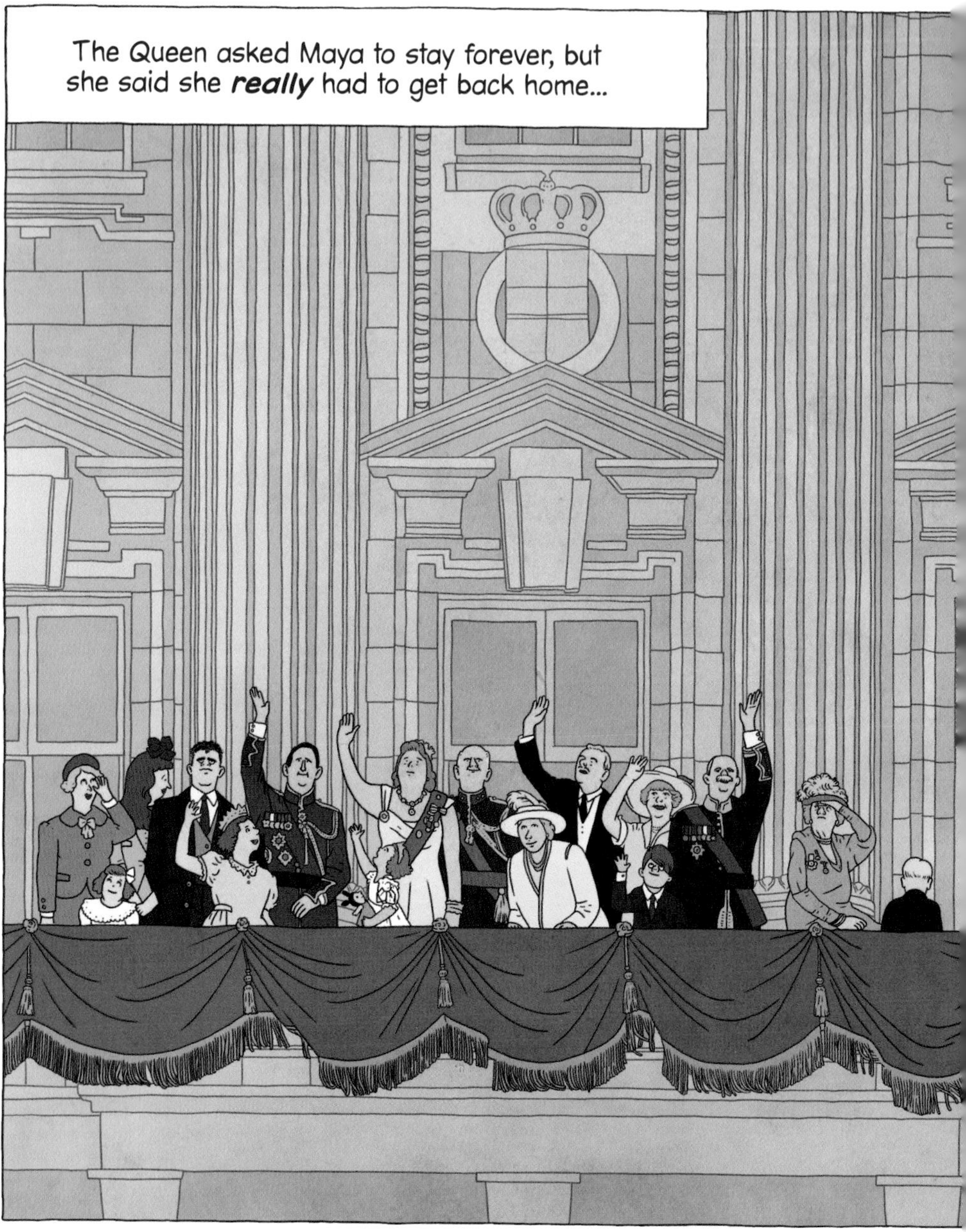
The Queen asked Maya to stay forever, but she said she ***really*** had to get back home...

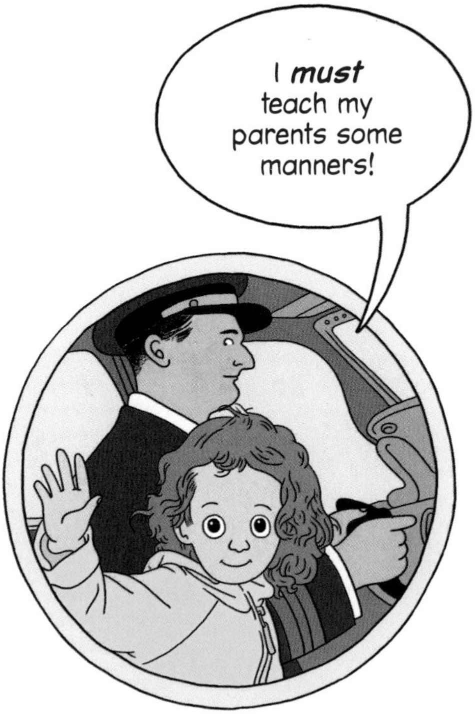
I ***must*** teach my parents some manners!

ABOUT THE AUTHOR

RUTU MODAN'S graphic novel, *Exit Wounds*, won the Eisner Award in 2008 and has been translated into 12 languages. And even though Rutu has received many awards for illustrating other authors' books, this is the first children's book she has written as well as drawn.

This book is a collaboration: When she was a child, Rutu liked ketchup so much she used to eat it with everything, even with cookies, or straight from the bottle (but only when her parents were not around). Then when Rutu's daughter, Michal, was young, she had very bad table manners. Rutu told her: "How badly you eat! What would you do if the Queen invited you to dine at the palace?" Michal answered very seriously: "Well! It just so happens that the Queen is a VERY good friend of mine, and she told me that I eat perfectly."

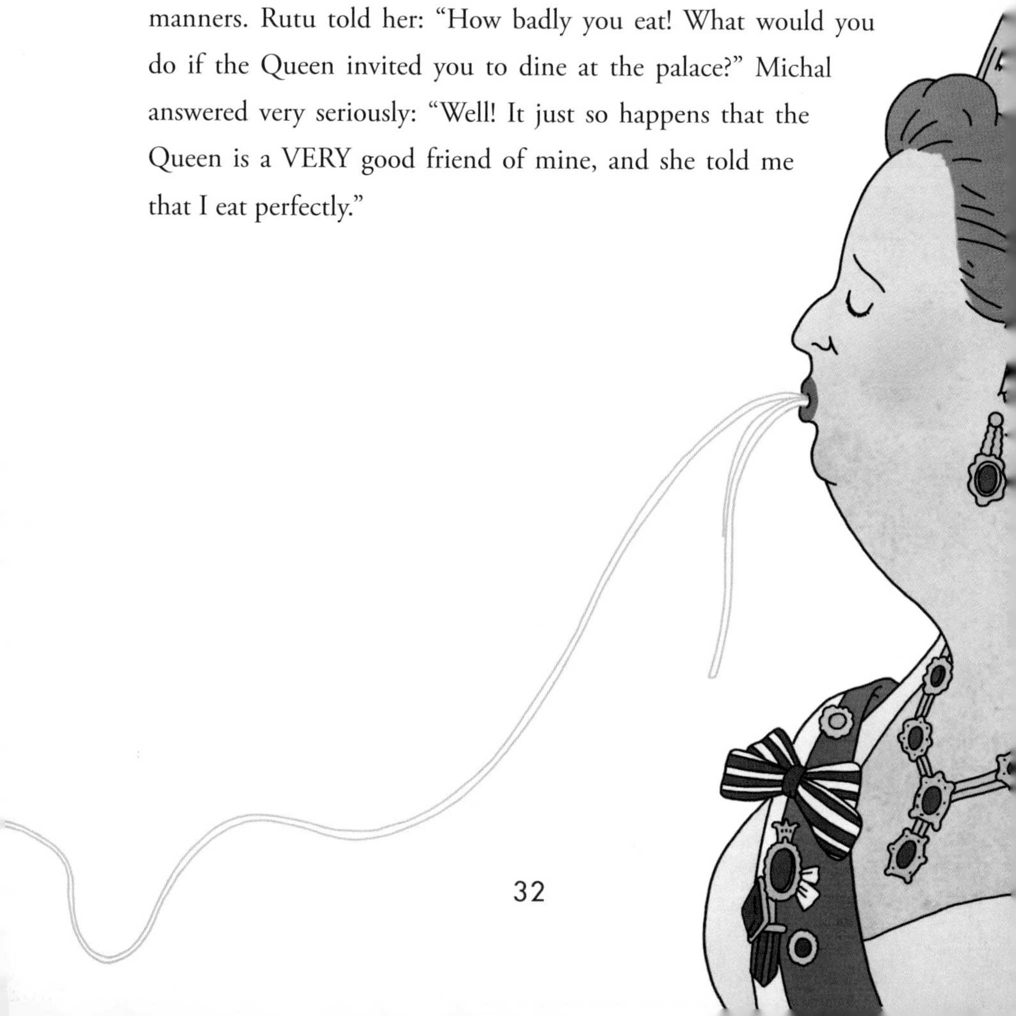

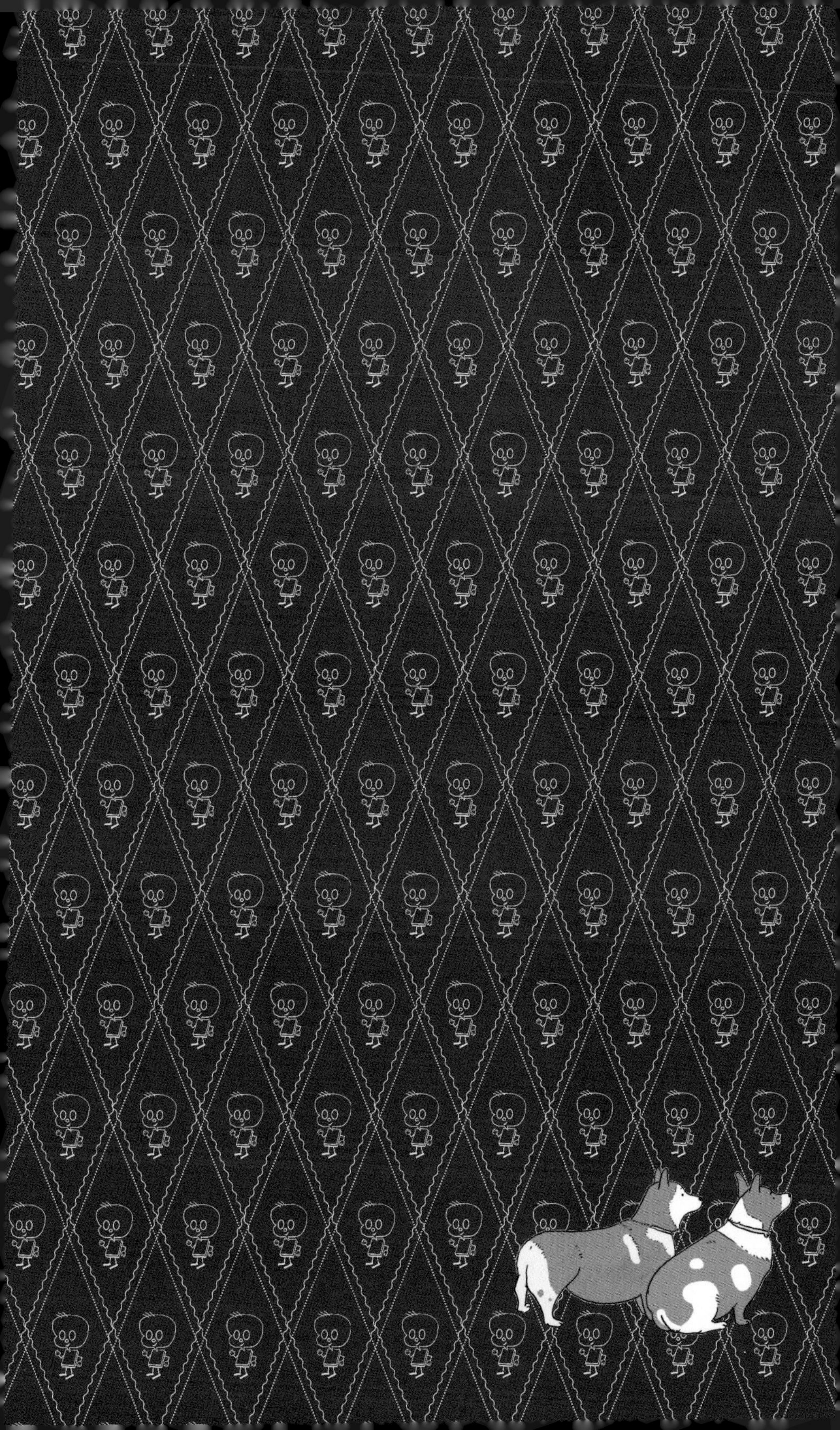

HOW TO READ COMICS WITH KIDS

Kids **love** comics! They are naturally drawn to the details in the pictures, which make them want to read the words. Comics beg for repeated readings and let both emerging and reluctant readers enjoy complex stories with a rich vocabulary. But since comics have their own grammar, here are a few tips for reading them with kids:

GUIDE YOUNG READERS: Use your finger to show your place in the text, but keep it at the bottom of the speaking character so it doesn't hide the very important facial expressions.

HAM IT UP! Think of the comic book story as a play and don't hesitate to read with expression and intonation. Assign parts or get kids to supply the sound effects, a great way to reinforce phonics skills.

LET THEM GUESS. Comics provide lots of context for the words, so emerging readers can make informed guesses. Like jigsaw puzzles, comics ask readers to make connections, so check a young audience's understanding by asking "What's this character thinking?" (but don't be surprised if a kid finds some of the comics' subtle details faster than you).

TALK ABOUT THE PICTURES. Point out how the artist paces the story with pauses (silent panels) or speeded-up action (a burst of short panels). Discuss how the size and shape of the panels carry meaning.

ABOVE ALL, ENJOY! There is of course never one right way to read, so go for the shared pleasure. Once children make the story happen in their imagination, they have discovered the thrill of reading, and you won't be able to stop them. At that point, just go get them more books, and more comics.

www.TOON-BOOKS.com

SEE OUR FREE ONLINE CARTOON MAKERS, LESSON PLANS, AND MUCH MORE

TOON into Reading

LEVEL 1

GRADES K–1

LEXILE BR–100 • GUIDED READING A–G • READING RECOVERY 7–10

FIRST COMICS FOR BRAND-NEW READERS

- 200–300 easy sight words
- short sentences
- often one character
- single time frame or theme
- 1–2 panels per page

LEVEL 2

GRADES 1–2

LEXILE BR–170 • GUIDED READING G–J • READING RECOVERY 11–17

EASY-TO-READ COMICS FOR EMERGING READERS

- 300–600 words
- short sentences and repetition
- story arc with few characters in a small world
- 1–4 panels per page

LEVEL 3

GRADES 2–3

LEXILE 150–300 • GUIDED READING J–N • READING RECOVERY 17–19

CHAPTER-BOOK COMICS FOR ADVANCED BEGINNERS

- 800–1000+ words in long sentences
- broad world as well as shifts in time and place
- long story divided in chapters
- reader needs to make connections and speculate

COLLECT THEM ALL

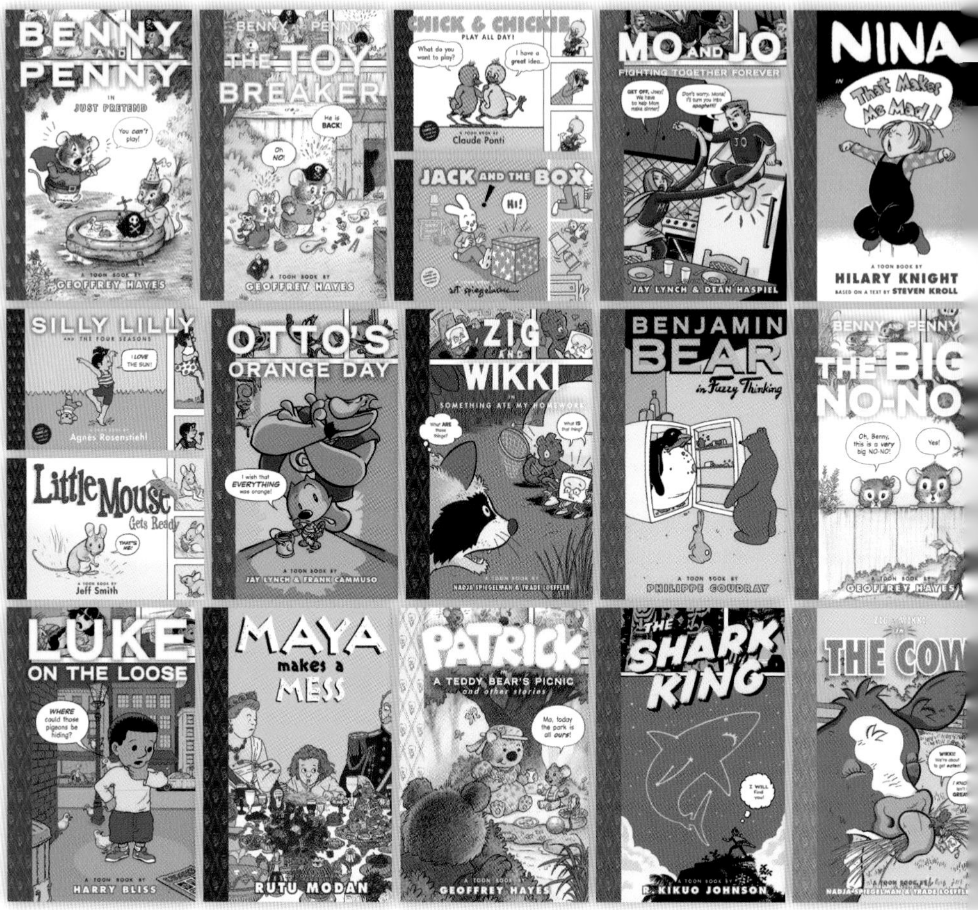
BENNY AND PENNY
IN JUST PRETEND
You can't play!
A TOON BOOK BY GEOFFREY HAYES
BENNY AND PENNY
THE TOY BREAKER
He is BACK!
Oh NO!
A TOON BOOK BY GEOFFREY HAYES
CHICK & CHICKIE
PLAY ALL DAY!
What do you want to play?
I have a great idea...
A TOON BOOK BY Claude Ponti
JACK AND THE BOX
HI!
art spiegelman
MO AND JO
FIGHTING TOGETHER FOREVER
JAY LYNCH & DEAN HASPIEL
NINA
IN
That Makes Me Mad!
A TOON BOOK BY HILARY KNIGHT
BASED ON A TEXT BY STEVEN KROLL
SILLY LILLY
AND THE FOUR SEASONS
I LOVE THE SUN!
Agnès Rosenstiehl
Little Mouse Gets Ready
THAT'S ME!
A TOON BOOK BY Jeff Smith
OTTO'S ORANGE DAY
I wish that EVERYTHING was orange!
A TOON BOOK BY JAY LYNCH & FRANK CAMMUSO
ZIG AND WIKKI
IN
SOMETHING ATE MY HOMEWORK
A TOON BOOK BY NADJA SPIEGELMAN & TRADE LOEFFLER
BENJAMIN BEAR
in Fuzzy Thinking
A TOON BOOK BY PHILIPPE COUDRAY
BENNY AND PENNY
THE BIG NO-NO
Oh, Benny, this is a very big NO-NO!
Yes!
A TOON BOOK BY GEOFFREY HAYES
LUKE ON THE LOOSE
WHERE could those pigeons be hiding?
A TOON BOOK BY HARRY BLISS
MAYA makes a MESS
RUTU MODAN
PATRICK
IN
A TEDDY BEAR'S PICNIC
and other stories
Ma, today the park is all ours!
A TOON BOOK BY GEOFFREY HAYES
THE SHARK KING
I WILL find you!
A TOON BOOK BY R. KIKUO JOHNSON
ZIG AND WIKKI
IN
THE COW
A TOON BOOK BY NADJA SPIEGELMAN & TRADE LOEFFLER

TOON BOOKS SET 1

Set of 10 hardcover books	**978-1-61479-298-7**
Benny and Penny in Just Pretend	978-1-61479-148-5
Benny and Penny in the Toy Breaker	978-1-61479-149-2
Chick & Chickie Play All Day!	978-1-61479-150-8
Jack and the Box	978-1-61479-151-5
Mo and Jo Fighting Together Forever	978-1-61479-152-2
Nina in That Makes Me Mad!	978-1-61479-153-9
Otto's Orange Day	978-1-61479-154-6
Silly Lilly and the Four Seasons	978-1-61479-155-3
Silly Lilly in What Will I Be Today?	978-1-61479-156-0
Zig and Wikki in Something Ate My Homework	978-1-61479-157-7

TOON BOOKS SET 2

Set of 8 hardcover books	**978-1-61479-298-**
Benjamin Bear in Fuzzy Thinking	978-1-61479-299-
Benny and Penny in the Big No-No!	978-1-61479-300-
Little Mouse Gets Ready	978-1-61479-301-
Luke on the Loose	978-1-61479-302-
Maya Makes a Mess	978-1-61479-303-
Patrick in a Teddy Bear's Picnic and Other Stories	978-1-61479-304-
The Shark King	978-1-61479-305-
Zig and Wikki in the Cow	978-1-61479-306-